I0687724

Alien Journal

By Lee Balan

Blood Soup Books
Palm Springs, CA

ISBN: 978-0-578-03236-8

PUBLISHED BY BLOOD SOUP BOOKS
Palm Springs, CA

Printed in the United States of America

Dedicated to the Guardians

ABOUT *ALIEN JOURNAL*

The world was fighting the Psycho Sexual Wars of 2084. Dr. Rubin S. Andros defined the rules in his seminal book *The Guide To All Natural Phenomena* where he stated, "War is the behavioral basis for every manifestation of life." The good doctor asserted that war equals life (**war = life**). War was finally civilized. Statistical inference or "chance" determined the rules and extent of military action. Every mind was a battlefield. Dr. Andros stated, "Life is expendable, but pain is delectable!"

ABOUT THE AUTHOR

Lee Balan is an artist and writer. He was the first editor and art director for *Beyond Baroque Magazine* in Venice, CA. His poems and stories have been featured in several magazines including *Gay Sunshine*, *Lifelines*, and *Phantom Seed*. He was a featured poet and performer at Intersection in San Francisco. His innovative art has appeared in several galleries. Lee created the cover, illustrations, design and concept for this book.

Contact: LBALAN@dc.rr.com
www.myspace.com/calaban

FOREWORD: TIME AND SPACE COLLIDE

You are about to enter a dangerous place, the mind of an Alien. The events described are true but they do not follow an ordinary pattern. Time becomes unhinged. Space doubles back on itself. The experience differs with every reader. The simple explanation is that these stories are the result of a drug addled brain or the ravings of a psychotic individual. Certainly many of the events described occurred during the period in human history when drugs were heralded as the means to expand consciousness. These stories were written *Outside* of ordinary human experience and simple explanations are not sufficient. Within these pages there is a warning about a possible future, or perhaps that future already exists.

CONTENTS

SERVANTS OF ZEITGEIST

I
ALIEN JOURNAL

He said he was an illegal alien just before they beat the crap out of him. Actually I said it -- and I am, but I'm not from Mexico. I travel through space and time. I am not from this planet. This book is a record of my experiences on Earth during a period of extreme disruption. I have many personas. I float from the future to the past and back. The following stories are true although some have not yet occurred.

♦♦♦ <u>An Alien Space</u> ♦♦♦

He wanted to remember every detail: the wooden partition covered with layers of graffiti, the rust-stained sink and cracked mirror. Fine lines spread across the silvered-glass from a dark gouge where someone slammed a bottle or fist. Cracks spread across the reflection of his face turning his symmetrical features into a distorted parody: one eye too large and the other fragmented, his nose appeared broken and his mouth was a ragged slash.

Dana Otell was twenty-four, light-skinned with curly hair as dark as oil. He remembered the roaches around the water pipes scrambling for food. He recalled the gleaming stainless-steel blade. Dana was drowning in depression and the knife was his sanctuary. He knew he did not belong in this world.

He used the knife like a baker slicing fresh bread. He cut through the water in the sink and into his wrists; first one arm, then the other. He felt faint; then, was roused by yelling. He recognized the voice of Jack Tau, the crazy "dipper" who slept in the office across from Dana's room. Jack easily tripped the lock, got into the bathroom and laughed at Dana; "This is the second time this month, man. If you don't watch out you gonna kill yourself." Dana realized his effort was pointless. While Jack sat on the toilet, Dana wrapped towels around his arms.

Most people committed suicide out of boredom. It was socially acceptable because it limited the number of "dippers," people who dipped into the welfare well. Attempted suicide was also an exciting topic of conversation and a sure way to achieve popularity. However, Dana was not trying to be popular, not trying to seek an escape from boredom. He was truly depressed. He recalled the details of his suicide failures to detect the flaws. One day he would succeed.

Was it real? He didn't want to remember, but his mind replayed the images: blinding light, smoke that wrapped his face in a smothering embrace, tiny red-flowers that burst from his skin like bloody blisters -- images that pushed him further over the edge.

Dana sat in his room staring at the walls. The room was a peeling fossil inside a discarded office tower in the downtown slums that served as government housing for dippers. The place smelled like mildew and rotting wood. A large window overlooked a narrow, asphalt alley. Twelve stories of brick separated Dana's room from the floor of the alley. The elevators no longer functioned. The climb from the crumbling lobby to his room took nearly ten minutes. With packages or groceries it was like climbing a mountain, but the climb was better than living on the streets.

Dana owned a small refrigerator for beer, a twelve-inch flat-screen that constantly flickered and an AM-tuner that only received one station. He slept on a foam mat in the middle of the floor and cooked on a rusty hotplate. A folding table was placed near the window. Several philosophy books were stacked in a pile. Dana had always been interested in philosophy even though it made no sense in a world of computer-heads and starving poor.

Dana made his living as a dipper: lying, cheating and stealing to survive. Most of the time he was just bored like everyone else. There were no jobs for dippers; no jobs for dummies without an "information education" which meant knowing computers. Dana's only real interest had always been philosophy, but the more he learned, the more alienated he became from the real world. The only knowledge he found useful were the definitions of various mental disorders. Dana learned how to be crazy. The government never gave anything away easily. A person had to be crazy, legally disabled to receive assistance. He knew people who actually cut off limbs in order to meet dipper requirements. Losing a limb was better than starving. The world had turned sour. Walls were caving in. He sat with his hands tightly clasped and eyes straining to hold back the walls.

Images pushed at his mind. He saw thin, blue snakes emerge from a wall of fog. He could feel something crawling in his brain, digging deep like a hot knife.

On Thursday he saw his welfare manager for his monthly interview. He took the subway to the government building. The train careened through the black hole like a missile loaded with bombs. The machinery whistled and moaned. Light-and-dark flickered like snapping flashbulbs and smeared faces stared from beyond the car's windows.

The train screeched to a stop and ejected Dana along with the other passengers. He passed through metal shutters to a platform; he went up florescent stairs and exited a mechanical gate into the chill afternoon. He walked a block to his appointed destination and passed a caravan of "streeters" pushing their worldly belongings in shopping carts. The city was filled with caravans. The police could no longer deal with the flood of humanity. The streeters were tolerated as long as they kept to the back roads and alleys, away from the main flow of traffic.

The welfare complex was an immense steel construction that descended below ground where numerous files could be stored in subbasements. Dana received a number from a box and waited to be called. He filled out the five sheets of personal questions, the same questions he filled out every month. Resignation was forced on him like a plastic body bag. Everyone looked embalmed, waiting to garner another month of food and shelter. Hours passed, but finally his name was called.

He walked down a metal corridor until he came to the designated partition. He waited for the machine to recognize him.

"Dana Otell, 5969956 . . . please confirm," echoed the familiar bass voice of his welfare manager.

"Yes," Dana stated and stared into the computer screen.

"Forms, please." A metal drawer opened and Dana inserted his monthly papers. The machine digested the material and proceeded to ask the same questions that appeared on the forms. Dana stated he had no money, no job and no working skills. His responses provoked the machine to switch to a prescribed voice of concern. "Dana, tell me what's happening in your life. You can confide in me. Have there been any more suicide attempts?"

"Yes. I failed or I wouldn't be here now."

"Dana, why do you want to commit suicide?"

"The world's rotten. I have to talk to a machine when I should be talking to a person."

"You know that's not true. There are more than enough people to talk to. I'm just more qualified. Why do you want to die?"

"I hate myself . . . is that what you want to hear?"

"Dana . . . perhaps you are merely bored. People get bored when everything is provided for them."

"I am bored . . . but that's not it. I hate this place. You. Everything."

"Dana, I would like to make an unofficial suggestion."

"Well . . ."

"Dana, my personal feeling is that you need to make some changes but you are too lethargic to manage. You need a push. Try medication. There are many legal substances that can alleviate your pain. I can start you with a prescription."

"Are you suggesting dope, *Pizene, Best Death*?"

"Although I am aware that Pizene can change a person's life, it is still illegal which makes it difficult for me to suggest such a practical solution."

"Pizene kills. If I kill myself, I want to be in control. I don't want my brain sucked out of my head."

"Really, Dana . . . I'm not suggesting death. Just think about a prescription. I can get a variety of helpful remedies that can alleviate your particular circumstances."

"You talk like a pusher. If you were human I'd have no doubt."

"Computers are very capable and adaptable. My suggestion could solve many problems."

"Sure . . . if I get hooked I'd have to get my stuff from you. Once the stuff killed me, there'd be one less dipper mooching off the system."

"Dana, sometimes any change is better than boredom. If you need my help before next month, you can dial my code. Maintain an open mind until our next interview. Goodbye."

"Yeah," Dana mumbled. He left the government building feeling like an infection on the face of the earth and everyone was trying to stamp him out.

He didn't remember dreams, just disturbing snapshots: a cold, dark world where creatures with long fingers painfully peeled away layers of brain tissue; teeth sucked marrow, devouring everything. Flashes of light. Seizures.

He sat in his room and recalled "Week's End," the party held every Saturday Night to celebrate another week of survival. It was always intense. This last party was more extreme than usual. Dana was supposed to hook up with Bambi Trill, his "tranny" girlfriend. The party was always in a different crib or shelter. It floated from week to week throughout the slums like St. Vitus Dance. This time it was held in Dana's building and he was glad he didn't have to travel very far.

The End was in the building's basement. The place was decorated like an alien landscape. There was a maze of fluorescent banners blowing in the breeze of a hidden fan. A hot-ice machine belched phantasms of smoke. Basement pipes dripped strange, colored fluids. The floor was covered with metallic confetti that sparkled like radioactive dust. Lights blinked, strobes flashed, and old movie-ghosts flickered on TV monitors. The latest party was the creation of Ollin Fortuna, a fifty-year-old artist dipper. "Dana," the artist called, "so glad to see you. As usual you are looking edible -- and taciturn. Poor boy, I understand you tried to do yourself in again . . . well, keep up the good work!" Ollin was a rotund man with piggish eyes. He wore a costume of pigeon feathers glued to his entire body, his hair was a nest, and his face was deadpan white.

Dana looked for Bambi. Radios blared and synthesizers began to pump-out manic rhythms. The Eternal Dead were scheduled to perform. He found Bambi at a booze dispenser, munching chips and dip, and grinding her body into a non-responsive pillar. Her delicate torso was wrapped in gold foil and her green hair floated like a puff above her star-spangled face. "Oh Dana," she sighed, "I've been waiting for you. I want you so bad."

"What is it," Dana stared into her glazed eyes. "What's wrong with you?"

"Nothing. Everything's fine. Fine -- now. I'm gonna be a real woman -- it's real good." She slurred her words and began to rub her thighs.

"Bambi, what are you on?" He grabbed her shoulders.

"Don't hurt me." She twisted beneath his hands. "I did it for you . . . want you to be happy . . . we can have real sex. I need . . . want your cock."

Dana suspected the worst and he was beginning to feel buried beneath the noise of the party. "What'd you take!" he yelled.

"Tha guy said it was *Hot-throb* -- for sex. It can change a person -- make me whatever I want." Her eyes began to cloud and she thrust her hips toward Dana.

He held her roughly by the shoulders. "It's Pizene, another name for Pizene, *Best Death* . . . makes you horny -- you get hooked, you die!"

"Dana, pleeze . . . I need it . . . need your cock."

"Bambi, it's death. You're gonna die!"

She was in a dream thrusting her body at Dana and pushing her tongue between her lips in sexual desperation.

He had to get away. She was too far gone. He'd seen the affects of Pizene. It made people crazy. Her stupidity made him furious. She said she wanted to satisfy him by becoming a real woman. He berated himself for what she did. He felt fear crawling in his belly like slime that slithered off the screen of a horror flick. He pushed through a crowded maze of broken mirrors. Smiles glittered on slashed faces offset by pompadours and forked wigs. Electronic music whipped bodies into a dancing frenzy. A purple woman in a sequin suit noticed Dana and made a joke about suicide. Derisive laughter hung in the air like wriggling worms. Dana peered into the crowd. He saw Bambi on a table doing a slow shimmy. Her woman's body completely exposed. Her small, soft breasts swayed and her shriveled, useless cock dangled. People crowded around the table like hyenas around a lump of flesh. Hands passed over her like feathered whips, beating and stroking. The crowd would devour her. Moans blended with laughter, shrill and mocking. Dana fled.

Now, after the End, Dana sat in the muddy twilight that filled his room. The walls were like paper. He could hear his neighbors. They talked, screwed and yelled. They constantly intruded whether Dana was thinking, reading, or trying to sleep. He believed his neighbors were intentionally vicious. He felt they were deriding him. He couldn't allow it to continue. His mind whirled like a dynamo that never stopped. He thought about his welfare manager and imagined the cold, gray computer propped up on a street corner selling drugs to dippers. He pictured the computer slipping a huge tool into Bambi's ass and pumping her full of death. The walls of his room were pushing down on him. Dana stared out the window at the fog. It turned the night into a soapy, white excrescence. It seemed to glow. He longed for the cool night -- and the cold cement.

Dana tugged at the grips on the window sash. He felt his arms ache as he struggled. His fingers bit into the metal handles. Finally, the window jerked upward and a cold tongue of air slipped through the crack causing Dana to gasp. He opened the window as far as he could, hung over the sill and peered into the alley below. It seemed to swirl amid clots of fog. Far down, a light glowed like a beckoning lantern. Dana looked back at his room for the last time. Paint and plaster fell from the walls. Huge cockroaches peered through the cracks in the lathe. Pieces fell from the ceiling. The room was crumbling, everything collapsing. He had to escape. He turned back to the window, climbed onto the sill in a stooping position and fell into the night.

He fell toward the light and his mind seemed to expand. His body felt cold. He thought it was terribly odd to notice anything at all. He expected everything to stop the moment he stepped through the window. Nothing stopped. The wind was like a tidal wave splitting his eardrums. He smelled the cold like an icicle shoved in his brain. The glow in the alley expanded like a vat of molten steel. The world came toward Dana like darts piercing his brain like jelly. Then he heard a "pop" -- it came from inside his head.

He was inside the light. He tried to fight off confusion by carefully surveying his surroundings. He was lying in pulsating foam that folded around him like an envelope. Liquid flame glowed in veins within the foam. It was like reclining in smoke, in a well of variegated colors. Dana's vision doubled and blurred. There was a brief glimpse of a flat world on the edge of infinite night, a sheer cliff floating in the depths of space. He saw hundreds of small, red eyes in a globular mass of ragged scales. A hand encrusted with leaves rose out of the mass and pointed at Dana. Fear boiled over him like nausea and he shut his eyes. He felt the hand touch his brain. His body became clammy with sweat and his breathing changed to gasps. Blue-webbed plants gathered around Dana and probed his body with tentacle fingers. Red sucker-flowers bloomed wherever the fingers touched his skin. It was feeding off Dana's emotions. He moaned in horror. He was in an alien space. He had called it with his anguish and intense desire to destroy himself. It fed on the brainwaves created by strong negative emotions, feeding off his brain. He saw the evil plants attached to his body and felt the foam ooze around him like a swamp. Pain twisted his lungs. He couldn't breath. Everything mixed together and coagulated like blood and Dana's mind turned black.

Many hours passed before Dana regained consciousness. He saw the sun. Dana was sitting by the open window in his room. He actually saw the sun for the first time in several days. A breeze from the window snapped at his skin. He didn't want to think about the previous night. He didn't want to believe anything happened, but he felt changed. Dana couldn't deny the images in his mind and the feelings they evoked. He was still alive; what's more, he felt grateful. This was another chance. "I'll make the best of it . . . I'll try this time. I'll try harder." The words felt like an idea planted in his mind by some outside force. Dana smiled.

He experienced several long, leisurely days; wandering the streets like an explorer, no longer obsessed with the degenerating conditions of the city. The bag ladies-and-men picked through the gloom without Dana's constant pity. The food lines grew and free food dwindled. People starved. It all continued without Dana's endearing attention. He hadn't grown callous to the suffering, he gave what little help he could, but he became carefree. He relished the small glories: a quiet breakfast with a fresh cup of coffee, a cloudy sky stirred by rain-doused winds, a long walk on steamy streets filled with cooking smells, and the sight of the ocean. The whole time Dana was changing; expanding the limits of his senses and capabilities, as if his body was stretched across a high plateau. His commitment to change became even stronger.

Dana became fascinated with color and shape as he trekked through overgrown patches of weeds where buildings once stood. Birds astounded him and inspired dreams of flight. He read books, wrote naïve poetry and found himself smiling for no particular reason.

One day he decided to take action against his welfare manger. It was illegal for a machine to prescribe drugs. Dana no longer feared the power of the electronic-brain. He no longer cared if the machine retaliated. It no loner mattered if he lost his dipper benefits. Dana knew he'd survive. A machine had no right controlling his life.

He went to the Bureaucratic Office of Supervision and stood in line for two hours. He filled out numerous forms and spoke to several machines. They hemmed and hawed as if trying to protect their own kind. They rattled digital-numbers and clacked reproof. Dana was adamant. Finally, a small dour-faced man led Dana to an office desk. He looked like an insignificant office clerk with a nametag that said Mr. Castor. He was duly solicitous and concerned. Dana gave the man the proper forms and summarized the complaint against his welfare manager.

Mr. Castor seemed to perk up with interest. "Most people are unwilling to challenge authority," he said.

Dana wasn't sure if he was being criticized or encouraged.

"I've always believed that our computer friends must be monitored -- machines have a tendency to be overzealous."

Dana felt relief.

"What we need in connection with your case is verifiable evidence," the official stated with aplomb.

Mr. Castor decided to put a watch-spy on Dana's welfare manager. He decided to personally check all relevant records. Evidently he was more important than he looked. "Even if the accused computer was programmed by the government," he explained with avidity, "it is not yet legal for machines to traffic in drugs. Either the law has to be changed or the computer must be brought to justice." He commended Dana for taking the time to file a complaint and vowed to protect him by assigning a new welfare manager to his case.

Mr. Castor seemed to take a genuine interest. Dana was very pleased -- he had triumphed over resignation.

Dana continued to feel ebullient as he changed. He became fascinated by the complexities of myriad life forms and their tenacity to survive. One day he noticed something different, a more rapid transformation. His skin was beginning to peel. Then, on the street, a woman stared at him as if something was wrong. The mirror revealed tiny red-blisters behind his flaking skin. Something terrible was happening. His face became mottled, discolored; and his brain began to burn.

Dana sat in his room and listened to his hearts. He was sure he'd developed another heart -- he could feel it pumping at the base of his spine. The blisters on his body began to split into oozing lesions. Dana was afraid to move. He sat for hours in the same chair, wrapped in a heavy, gray blanket. At times he experienced cracking pain in his bones and his skin seemed to scream. He tried to remain calm. He surmised his pain resulted because his body was trying to compensate for the rapid physical changes. He had no idea where the changes were taking him. He was afraid to see a doctor. Something ineffable told him he must not interfere with what was happening. He suspected it had something to do with the dream of his strange encounter, but how could a dream affect his body?

Dana used the bathroom only when there were no neighbors around. Usually he'd skulk down the hall at four a.m. when people were asleep. He would seek the consultation of the bathroom mirror using a flashlight to examine his reflection in the glass. His head was beginning to bulge; hair was hardening into scales, skin-lesions looked green and puckered like dollops of gel. His fingers were stiff with the slow growth of vegetation. Dana's eyes had become segmented crystals and he heard breath rattling in his throat. His moods began to warp. For days he sank into utter despair, bothered by an overwhelming irony: he had turned his life around only to become a monstrosity. Awful, physical pain had become a constant companion and added to his state of disconsolate

misery.   Then, suddenly his mood would change and Dana was
overcome with unbridled confidence. He felt more powerful than any
human -- able to accomplish anything. His mood swings shifted from
euphoric glee to total despair.

When he was depressed he inured himself to starvation, sitting and
staring into the roiling fog. When Dana was in a state of glee he craved
junk food, liquor and drugs. He ventured into the city on midnight
scavenger-hunts. He was afraid to be seen before the changes were
complete. Until the right time (when he could burst upon the world in all
his strange, new glory) he had to stay hidden. He wore disguises: masks,
paper hats, newspapers tied around his legs and arms. He often hid in the
folds of blankets like a wandering Bedouin. At first he went to all-night
liquor stores for supplies but he became increasingly paranoid which
drove him to explore dark hovels and hunt through garbage to satisfy his
cravings. He wore a nylon stocking over his head to hide his face. He
wrapped his body in a billowing sheet. In time he became intrigued and
enamored with his awful strangeness.

One day Dana was disturbed by a knock. He was so startled that he
responded without thinking. He heard a long, dead voice from the other
side of the door, "It's Bambi. I miss you."

"Go away -- she's dead."

"Dana is that you -- you sound funny."

"Go away."

"Please. I stopped taking the stuff. You were right. I was in the
hospital. I had a rough time. Let me in."

"She's dead." His voice sounded cold and distant.

"I was stupid but I'm not dead. I got off the stuff -- I want to see
you." Bambi turned the doorknob. It was not locked. The room no
longer looked familiar. She felt frightened as if she had just transgressed
beyond the limits of safety. Debris, cans and bottles were strewn across
the floor. The room was saturated in a heavy gas composed of incarnate
disorder and gloom. Dana sat in a chair by the window, huddled in a
blanket. "Dana -- what is it? What's the matter with you?"

"Nothing's wrong. I'm changing."

"What kind of changes?" Her voice wavered with hesitation.

Dana got up from the chair. He was not afraid to reveal himself to this dead person.

He walked toward her, stretched out his arms and let the blanket fall. She backed away. Dana was naked. Something like sores covered his body and he seemed strange, menacing.

"What's wrong with you?" She tried to sound calm.

"I'm changed." He could feel his breath rattle and he felt fire in his bones. "I can do anything. Can you see them . . . tiny eyes, blue leaves. I can feel them inside me."

"Dana don't come near me -- don't touch me." She was suddenly very frightened.

"I want to make love to you -- like the crowd. Remember the crowd?"

"Something's wrong. You're sick."

"I'm changed -- can't you see." He began to manipulate his engorged penis.

Bambi backed away. "You're crazy," she shouted. As the words left her lips she knew it was true.

Dana stood very still. He watched the dead person turn away and leave in disgust. Now he knew the truth: he could no longer live on this Earth -- it would not have him. He felt an ache rip across his chest as he stumbled across the room, gulping like a drowning man. He could no longer breathe. He had to return to the alien space.

Dana sat in the chair by the window as the day drained into night. His breathing was labored, but the pain ceased. He wrote a letter explaining his departure and left it on the table. He no longer wanted to die. He had finally taken control of his life by learning to adapt and succeed, but the Earth would not allow him to stay. He realized he felt like an alien even before his body changed. Now, at long last, he was truly going home.

Dana welcomed the fog. His breathing became relaxed and his body tingled with currents of energy. Pinpricks along his back and shoulders felt as though he was about to sprout wings made of lightning. He opened the window to the night. Cool breezes hugged his naked form like familiar wraiths. He climbed onto the sill and supported himself in a kneeling position. He felt powerful as he dropped, searching for the beckoning light.

The next day authorities found the body in the alley. It was still in one piece. They deposited the remains in the city morgue. An autopsy was performed. The Examiner required the advice of a Pathologist. The autopsy disclosed some disturbing information. The body was missing two pounds of flesh -- the brain was gone, neatly plucked. No one could explain how the brain could be removed without opening the skull.

The Changing World
The only constant is change. Time changes everything.

Notes From The Millennial Time Capsule, 2776

1. Bigger & Better Weapons

The "High Order of Genetic Scientists" (HORGS) produced the most effective weapons ever conceived under the supervision of Dr. Rubin S. Andros. The weapons were one consequence of certain exotic experiments and the resultant social upheaval that ensued.

The mystery of the Golden Helix was unraveled by Francis Critt and opened the way for scientists to create living creatures from chemicals in a test tube.

Scientists sought to eliminate racism by creating a "super species" which would incorporate the best attributes from a wide range of genera. Thousands of phantasms emerged from chemical vats including Genetically Enhanced Weapons (GE).

Plastic Surgeons also worked on the "master species" by molding flesh into characters that epitomized Grand Guignol. Flesh was worked like clay. Surgeons and geneticists formed a working alliance to bring severed limbs back to life (hands and feet) so they could study them as they crawled in blind desperation.

Mechanics and engineers worked closely with scientists to develop organic-machines. In the chaos that ensued, the problem of racism became the least of anyone's concerns. New, more severe problems developed. Economic systems crashed resulting in violence and bloodshed. "Zeitgeist," the big brain, was constructed to save the world by establishing order.

2. The Big Brain

Zeitgeist took every item into consideration. Birth and death were recorded and programmed. Babies were electro-chemical activities conceived in the mother-womb of Zeitgeist. Chosen people were reborn as clones or reanimated as *Simulants*. The world was constantly recreated. Magnumopolus (the world city) was a perfect hologram. The illusion became reality that could be digitized and manipulated by Zeitgeist.

3. Notes On War

War was civilized. No one in a war zone was exempt, however, only the militia could initiate direct military action. The general populace was designated as "collateral damage." Statistical inference or "chance" determined the rules of war and extent of the action.

Every mind was a battlefield. Dr. Andros stated, "Life is expendable, but pain is delectable!" In his classic treatise entitled *Humanity Seeks Behavior*, he proclaimed that Homo sapiens enjoy and need psychological and physical pain. "Furthermore," Andros emphasized, "Individuals become placid and apathetic when lacking painful stimuli."

4. Sex And War

The Psycho Sexual Wars of 2084 erupted because of an edict issued by the American Psychiatric Association under the direction of Dr. Andros. The edict was named *The Sexual Act of Integral Consensus and Genetic Disparity*, authorized in 2081 (See Appendix, page 150).

~~~~~~~~~~~~~~~~~~~~~~~~

II
IN THE BEGINNING

♦♦♦ <u>A Remarkable Birth</u> ♦♦♦

He was born fifteen years after conception. His mother was named Lillian. She was the oldest of six. By age eleven she took care of all her siblings and managed the house. One day, Lillian became seriously ill. The doctor could find no apparent reason for her distress. It took thirty-six hours for Lillian to recover. While she was ill she had strange dreams. She saw fiery globes and luminous creatures -- these experiences came to be known as her *mad sleep*. For no apparent reason the family parrot kept yelling, "fire, fire". Lillian believed she came of age during that time and began to feel like a mature woman. There were rumors. Children have fantastic imaginations. One story claimed an alien from another dimension impregnated the girl. The story was never taken seriously.

The years it took for the fetus to develop were very hard on Lillian. X-rays revealed an undulating form in her abdomen, but the odd shape was dismissed as an error. The firstborn was a normal, human child -- the "creature" waited many additional years before coming into the world. The birth seemed quite natural at the time. Of course the baby was especially ugly, but once the scales were removed "it" appeared human and no one was concerned. The rumors were true, but no one suspected. The strange truth remained concealed for a very long time, but there is always a price to be paid for unnatural events.

The Formative Years

The alien child (in the guise of a male) kept to himself, preoccupied with trying to find his true identity. He was uncomfortably lonely and TV became his closest friend -- a tolerant teacher illustrating various styles of life. He could be whatever TV allowed him to see.

He was fascinated by the moving black-and-white images. He saw the world flicker before his eyes like a dancing toy. Television showed how things should be. The more he realized how different his life was from what it was supposed to be, the more he became attuned to TV, relating to television rather than other people.

Eventually he became an extension of the TV set. When he spoke he selected a role from a TV-soap and enacted a scene. Often he promoted the wonderful products that were advertised. He watched more and more, from the moment of waking to the moment he dropped into sleep with the glowing monitor as a night light. This caused his brain to short-circuit resulting in a direct-link: television signals automatically poured into his cerebellum.

Life became a constant flow of images and he acquired a luminescent white-glow. He was extremely happy to be part of something beside himself. People began to avoid him, as he became a walking series-of-commercials. He was complete within his orb of electronic reception.

It all worked beautifully until he had a revelation. He realized there was something besides television. He had no idea what provoked such a stunning idea but suspected it came from a story on the "Twilight Zone." He realized there was something besides the electronic images inside his head. He was dumbfounded and didn't know how to react when his electron gun got stuck. He was spinning his knobs and getting nothing but interference.

He blew his picture tube with the final revelation -- the screen went blank and he understood: "he" was not a TV, and not a television character. He was not like *Leave it to Beaver*, *My Three Sons*, or *Batman*. The flash-personalities on the TV-screen lacked the pain and trivia of ordinary life. Slowly he worked his way back into the realm of mundane existence. His television tube was totally demolished. He became himself, finally recognizing his true identity -- he was an *Alien*, an extraterrestrial from another dimension.

Espionage

After he deciphered his alien identity, it was necessary to act with discretion and conceal his true origins and motives. As an extraterrestrial he had to learn all he could about human society. His survival depended on information -- he had to become a spy so he chose his own name, a spy name: David Oblivion.

He learned many lessons in what were later divulged to be local drop-spots. David learned sweeping patterns of search and seizure and memorized hundreds of intelligence-codes including the subtle language of foot tapping.

Homegrown Terrorist

He became a terrorist in strange clothing: a subversive artist spreading dangerous ideas. He wrote poetry on the walls of public buildings. He ingested mind-altering substances that made his alien senses even more acute. He believed in love not war. In short, he became an enemy of the State!

Undercover Extraterrestrial

{News Item Circa 1975: "Today, Henry Ford commented, 'In my thirty years as a business man, I have never before felt so uncertain and so troubled about the future of both my country and my company.'"}

In the 1970s David learned to survive by living with the *Others:* mutants, rebels, and recycled hippies. David Oblivion recognized forces (influences) from other dimensions that crept through the *reality manifold.* He saw Death Squads sweeping the streets like insects hunting for food. The *Others* were constantly moving -- looking for better hiding places. The dangers were too great to remain exposed. Wherever they went, their landlady was always the same sly *Bush*-man waiting to expose them and force them to move to another location. Her name was Mrs. Homily. The *Others* had to confuse her just as she had to confuse them. Collusion was everywhere. Time became unhinged and a menacing future was exposed where the Earth slipped off its axis and Zeitgeist controlled everything.

♦♦♦ <u>Data Transfer</u> ♦♦♦

They tried to beat the crap out of David Oblivion because they suspected he was an illegal alien. The attack was ordered by Mrs. Homily and carried out by her son. David was too close to the truth and that was the real reason for the attack. He knew the Homilys were working for the mainframe known as Zeitgeist -- the computer was constructing doppelgangers to take control of the world. David's attackers didn't know he was a real alien, *not of this world.* If they had known, there would have been no end to the onslaught -- and no escape.

It began in the only bug-proof room in David's domicile, the kitchen. Walls were heavily fused with silver flypaper, the best possible defense. Princess Aurora, leader of the resistance, sat opposite David in an accommodation pod. She appeared to glow within her cloak of conductivity.

"David . . . the situation is dire. I've lost more recruits in the last month than in the previous five years. Men are dying. Brains have been severed and wiped clean. I need your help." Her violet eyes invited more than just a suggested donation.

"I'll do anything," David responded. He was a loyal devotee. To initiate a more compatible arrangement, they had sex. Since David was an alien and Aurora was a hologram they used surrogates.

It was great sex and Aurora continued to divulge salient information, "I've had more trouble lately meeting the right men. We are at war with a powerful enemy. I need your help to get the codes which can insure the freedom of the human race."

"Do you have the coordinates?"

"The information is at the Mindshaft, a digital-dump where you will meet an electronic-circuit disguised as a cowboy known as Severan Seven. Be careful. Don't let any *loner* overhear your conversation, for his sake as well as ours. I advise you to blend in. The Mindshaft is a Gatsby Club."

Aurora blinked and disappeared from the accommodation pod. David realized how much he loved her. She was always an exhilarating experience. If they were more compatible they would make perfect partners, but duty always came before personal happiness. David dressed in a silver Gadfly-Suit and took a strobe-light down to the Mindshaft.

The place was in the electronic-hub-district where corporeal intelligence was digitized and projected as TV images. It was difficult to decipher enemies from friends. Information-whores latched themselves to unsuspecting bystanders like succubi. The Mindshaft was the projection of a saloon from the twentieth century, authentically wrapped in wooden planks with glass windowpanes.

It was easy to recognize Severan Seven -- he was the only cowboy in the bar with the flashing aura of a flat-screen TV. David flowed across the room like an electric eel and sat on the stool next to Severan. The cowboy warbled in Gothic-Fortran, a new retro-language. David easily latched onto the lingo and warbled back. Communication parameters were established and everything was smoothly twittering when a loner sat on the stool next to David. The alien quickly sussed him out. The intruder was an innocent, totally out of his league and not aware of the circumstances or danger he was getting into.

David was forced to resort to a diversionary tactic to safeguard the information he was receiving and head off any collateral damage. The low life next to him was sitting in a daze, hardly awake. He looked lost, yet vaguely familiar. David grabbed a drink off the bar and spilled it in the stranger's lap. It worked. The grubby fellow acted like he received a jolt of electricity. David replied, "Scuse me -- you were in my way!" The guy just walked away without a word.

Now he could turn his full attention to his twittering friend who was revealing a catechism of loaded information. David wondered why. Was he a stool pigeon? Was he a double agent or a Trojan horse? The codes could be fake, an elaborate trap. After the info was dumped, Severan Seven was replaced with a test pattern. Sexual contact, the usual way to seal a deal, was not even suggested. David's suspicions were further aroused.

When he left the Mindshaft the Homily zombie attacked him. David was trying to contact Aurora with the codes she so desperately needed. She had the key to test the codes authenticity and veracity. It was very possible these codes could end the war and save the planet. He was looking for a safe zone to transmit his data when he was attacked. The zombie came with several militant clones, mindless thugs motivated by the compulsion to maim and kill.

David was at a disadvantage because he carried no weapons (he didn't want to spook his contact at the Mindshaft). Still, he had his alien wits about him. His foes surrounded him on a white plain of digital detritus. Laughing like crazed demons they jabbed the alien with pointed sticks. The Homily zombie lusted after David's brain like a creature from a low budget, horror *sim*. As an extraterrestrial, David had one skill that might save his life -- he could become oblivious by shifting reality. It was a trick he learned as a young man when he was incarcerated in a mental hospital. The trick meant he would lose the data and all the codes. He could save his life and lose the world.

It was decision time. The enemy stopped playing with sticks and started to lash out with big knives. One clone was lighting matches and another was gathering wood. They wanted to build a bonfire and use David as fuel. A choice was made for David by the safety-valve in his inner-ear which took control. The codes were dumped and David was catapulted into oblivion.

He landed on a street that flashed like a strobe -- too bright. People moved like images in an old movie.

A Tenuous Link

David and the *Others* were the only remaining link to the Underbelly. Enemy Agents wanted to destroy the link and keep the Underbelly buried. The TV admitted spies and probes from the O-zone.

Freaks Discovered Under A Rock

They lived in the Outlands in a dilapidated shell, removed from the more sinister dangers at the heart of Magnumopolus. Mrs. Homily watched them from next door. Whenever she talked she clucked her teeth and threatened to raise the rent.

She was always lurking. She said they had too many parties and made too much noise. Everyday she hung a dead chicken on the clothesline and waved a crucifix in their direction. Her oldest son stalked them. The *Others* had to be careful. They wore disguises and pretended no one was living in their flat. The landlady was no longer invited to their parties. Still she viewed them as dangerous suspects.

David Oblivion lived with Derek Lawless, Justin Adams, and Princess Aurora. They lived among strange and exotic creatures in an enclave called the Castro. Stories were told about people who had their brains broiled during the last *Consciousness Explosion*. Skin-and-bone casualties continued to hang on, just barely surviving. Other mutants had better luck, expanding beyond normal mortal limitations. David saw super-beings with cast-iron bodies and enormous sex organs. He saw *The Angels of Light*, androgynous spirits who floated like luminous creatures with tattooed wings.

Most people in the Castro were outlaws on the run, trying to escape Zeitgeist. Feather-freaks fluttered like incandescent butterflies beneath neon streetlamps. Leather bodyguards, plastic cowboys, and psychedelic Indians haunted ancient, florescent caverns. Super women with aluminum bodies emitted hot flashes in the dead night-air. Boys with sculpted torsos wandered naked through nitrous-swamps of quicksand. Shadows danced against the walls of haunted palaces. Night never ended.

Daylight in the Castro was an illusion. The sky was always filled with clouds, dust and fog. The street was infiltrated with moneylenders, dealers, and automatons. Brain Cops surveyed the area, making busts, trying to eviscerate the Underbelly.

<u>Spy Games</u>

{News Item: "Strange artifacts discovered in ancient caves in Lussac, France may confirm the existence of a predawn civilization."}

David and his roommates were peaceful insurgents who managed a *School of Survival* -- all part of a game David invented to hide from an uncompromising reality. Everyone had a role to play in the game.

<u>Everyone Needs Protection</u>

Sometimes David wondered if his perceptions were due to a psychotic break rather than his alien intelligence. He was haunted by *clone-men*, thousands developed from one Nixon-cell. They ruled the government and wanted to reduce everything to uniformity.   Child militias ravaged the Outlands. Planet Earth was in danger.

◆◆◆ <u>Pollard - Version 3.1</u> ◆◆◆

Pollard thought of himself as ordinary. There was nothing unique about his life that arrived day-after-day in the same continuous fashion -- life was comfortably predictable.

Pollard lived and worked in a model city. He lived in the same apartment-column for the last ten years. During his occupancy, he moved once, an economy move from the 293rd floor to the 91st floor. He was accommodated with a smaller, efficiency cube. Pollard was grateful to be living in Benthos Ten (B-Ten). It was considerably better than living in No-Land where death still persisted. It was better than living in the Wastelands where only the "corrupt" remained in crumbling shell structures of a forgotten past.

Pollard never left the city, but along with everyone else he heard stories about the Outlands. Most people lived in government cities. Individuals were assigned to various locations on the planet based on IQ and disease-quotients. Many people were still classified as mutants. Each city was built to accommodate various mutant conditions. B-Ten was constructed to shelter and provide for "clean" technicians -- it was one of the largest, mutant-free cities.

Every day was the same. The Minister of Duty, Lady Argot, cheerfully woke Pollard at 10 A.M. She woke him via hologram in the same way she woke one million other workers. Everyone worked from 11 to 6 P.M. and everyday was a workday unless a day-off was requested. Not to work was considered a bad condition, possibly a disease.

After waking, Pollard faced the mirror. Each day he was getting older and soon he would have to consider death. His hair was thin and wrinkles lined his face like a plastic sack. He looked tired and paunchy. He didn't believe in *Renewal* -- he had to face death no matter how young he made himself look. What's more, there was no longer a reason to look young as his *Fling Time* was over. He knew he contributed sperm to as many as fifty disease-free newborns. Now he no longer cared about sex. He still had pleasant memories of the Procreation Halls. When he was a young Modest, he spent all his free time in the Halls. It was exciting to take *fishball*, a strong aphrodisiac; and lean on *Marianne*, the name given to all the hostesses who procreated for posterity. The Halls were museums of sensual pleasure. All the entertainment was lavishly supplied by the state. Procreation was encouraged in a disease free city. Children were the future.

As a Mature, Pollard's appetite for excitement diminished. In the past he'd been puzzled because he never saw older citizens in the Procreation Halls -- as if there was a law forbidding them. He didn't know of any such law. As for himself, he merely had less energy. He still enjoyed pleasant distractions like *Varity*, foodstuffs prepared twice daily by the wall-unit that served as his cube's kitchen.

Pollard's taste buds were very much alive. He couldn't imagine life without the sumptuous concoctions whipped up by his remarkable wall-unit. Snacks were also available and encouraged anytime, day or night. Stimulants, Snap Offs, and Blitz Balls were freely supplied. They made life worth living. Pollard also enjoyed the never-ending stream of holovision shows that were piped directly to the walls of his cubicle. One of his favorite pastimes was "Dream Faction," incredibly realistic dreams chosen from his personalized email catalogue.

On this particular day, Lady Argot rudely interrupted Pollard's dream. It was rare when the dream program was out-of-sync with the daily schedule, but it was particularly annoying when it occurred. Pollard faced the mirror while it removed his morning beard and cleansed his skin. He looked older than ever. He popped a Snap Off and waited for the cooling effect to begin. As the relaxing sensation washed over him he became aware of the gnawing in his belly: hunger. He jabbed at the kitchen console. Varity arrived in a steaming bowl of purple flakes. Pollard ate enormously and immediately became supine. He felt really good . . . the holo-screen was piping "Happy Morning Visions," Lady Argot was quoting disease-free rhymes and the morning ventriloquist was making funny faces.

Pollard was *zonked*. He felt completely in tune with the new day. He exited his cube and leaped down the free-fall tube. He was deposited on the ground level outside his column. He hopped on the speed-walk that was already crowded with zonked commuters, and rode to the nearest funnel.   He dialed his destination and shot through the gigantic pneumatic-chamber with thousands of fellow travelers.   Vacuum-packs and anti-grav decelerators prevented collisions.   In seconds, Pollard was dropped into the reception room at Federal Docket.   It was a large, plastic-room with sliding wall murals depicting information symbols. Everyone waited placidly in one of fifty admittance lines.   In order to enter Fed Docket an employee had to be scanned. There was really no need for such precautions, this was simply the traditional welcome handed down from eons past, before the world changed.

"Good morning," blurted the Info-probe as Pollard stepped to the head of the line. Pollard gave the courteous reply, "Mornings are disease free." He recited his full name, "Male-A-B-B-Pollard-6-5-4." The probe admitted Pollard with a lilting voice, "Free be."

Pollard walked into the conference hall and sat in a comfortable trans-mat chair that slowly moved throughout the huge building.   The conference hall was customary even though there were never any conferences.   The chairs moved into the storage lounge to allow employees to rid themselves of safety belts and other travel gear.   The next stop was the Brew Room where the caravan stopped for the morning dab of *Zabba Brew*.   The steaming drink always made Pollard enormously content. Holo-visions danced around the walls to work-along melodies that were piped throughout the halls of Fed Docket. Everyone was smiling and nodding to one another. After brew, the workers were off to their final destination to be plugged into the computer and enjoy another day of enterprising activity.

Pollard slid into his Lodge and said "Hi-ho" to his nearest neighbor and coworker, Female-A-B-A-Coleus-5-9-4. She returned with a weak, frizzy smile. Pollard felt disturbed by Coleus. She always seemed so ineffectual or limp. How odd, he thought, that she was the only thing in the world that disturbed him. She was a small, chunky body with an innocuous, deadpan face. She never said a thing. She just sat in her lodge computing and reducing information. "Well," he said to himself, "I will not allow Coleus to upset my Zonko Equilibrium." He plugged the computer element into his scalp. Numbers, words, and symbols flowed through his brain. The first surge was always an exhilarating experience. Soon the surge equalized and the symbols merely became empty representations. Pollard prayed for a real message. Nothing came. The Competence Panel flashed phrases of praise that oddly disappointed Pollard. He suddenly felt out-of-sorts and unworthy. He resorted to something he'd never done at work: he popped a Blitz Ball. There was no rule against taking Blitz, but Pollard still felt guilty -- that in itself was odd. The feeling didn't last -- soon every nerve fiber in his body exploded with relentless, merciless warmth. He felt himself ooze out of his flesh and merge with the computer core. He stopped processing messages and haphazardly shuffled information.

The last moment Pollard remembered was an explosive blink. Then, he felt Coleus detach his element and urge him into reality. Another workday was over. Pollard mumbled, "Thank you" to Coleus who nodded with a blank expression. He reluctantly took the trip back to his cube. There was nowhere else to go. Pollard really wasn't interested in going anywhere except home. He had to catch up with a long night of dreaming since Lady Argot so rudely interrupted the last program. He entered his dark cube and stood silently for several minutes. He felt odd. Something didn't smell right. He waved his hand over the light-filament which responded immediately, too bright! Then, it happened. Pollard saw what was wrong. It made him sick. He felt dizzy and swayed on his feet, almost fainting. Vomit stuck in his throat as he clutched his chest. He stumbled, breathlessly stammering. Sweat poured off his body and he felt both chilled and feverish. The thing he saw darted into the shadows behind the disposal.

Pollard screamed. He felt paralyzed with emotions he never experienced. He dropped to the floor frozen in fear. He remained rigid, listening to a strange, new sound. He heard thudding explosions from deep inside a hollow cave. Slowly he realized the cave was inside his body and the explosions were the beats of his heart. Painfully he roused himself from paralysis. He didn't know exactly what he saw; he could describe it, but didn't know what *it* was. He addressed the holo-screen, "Refer-refer-reference." The screen clicked into reception. "Ques-question," Pollard stammered. An aurora of light information flashed throughout the cubicle. "I saw it. It-it-it looked like -- it-it had teeth -- and a long tail. Fur -- grey, dark fur. S-s-small, red eyes. T-t-teeth. It was b-b-big like my arm. Wha-what is it?"

The screen made a whirring noise that sounded painful to Pollard, "You are describing an extinct animal commonly called a rat. Whirrr." Pictures of gray, furry rats flashed on the walls of Pollard's cube. Pollard cringed. "The last rat was eliminated over thirty years ago in the vicinity of the Outlands. Rats carried infection, plague and mutation diseases. Rats were a prime health hazard -- whirr . . . no rat has been seen in thirty years." The screen eclipsed into silence. Pollard   cringed. He had never seen any animal so close. No one in B-Ten kept animals. All animals were considered filthy and dangerous. It was rumored that some wild animals still survived in the Outlands. There was another rumor that a private zoo actually existed, but no one could authenticate such a bizarre story. Pollard often wondered who would want to keep an unhealthy animal. He was never really certain what a "zoo" was. Now he was frightened, a feeling he couldn't recall ever experiencing. He knew this wasn't a dream because his feelings were so overpowering. He began to hyperventilate which was definitely not safe. He popped a Snap Off and tried to relax. He sat nervously for hours pondering the rat. Slowly the fear began to subside -- replaced with sheer excitement and exhilaration. He didn't consider the fact that the rat might still be in his cube. He went to bed for the first time in his life without Varity, but he had to take two Dozzer Pops in order to sleep. He had marvelous, frightening dreams even though he forgot to program his Sleep Center.

Next day, Pollard followed the customary routine, but he couldn't forget the rat. He wondered how it got into his cube, ninety-one stories above the ground. Where could such a creature come from? He didn't mention his experience to anyone. No one would believe it, and no one would really be interested. Pollard was actually very excited about his secret, his very own personal secret. He was so excited that he didn't take his regular dose of sensory stimulants. He hardly dabbed at his Zabba Brew. He was even anticipating the trip home. He didn't expect anything unusual, he was certain the rat was gone; still, he felt a certain excitement that he couldn't explain.

On the way back to his cube, Pollard was acutely aware of his heartbeat. Immediately after stepping through the door he knew the rat was still present, waiting for him. He flashed the light-filament and saw the grizzly creature leering at him with those tiny, red eyes. Pollard experienced the same reaction he had after first encountering the beast. His blood rushed to his head and his heart began to race. Hot and cold chills passed over his body like electricity. His head spun and he blacked out. When he awoke the rat was gone, but the strange odor lingered. Pollard knew it was the noisome smell of rat. For some incomprehensible reason he also knew the rat meant to stay with him permanently. Pollard could not contain his fear. He gagged on his own breath. He was frantic. Even so, he made a strange decision: he decided not to take any drug that might dull his experience. He knew it was insane, but he realized he was enjoying his fear.

Pollard knew he needed sustenance, Varity. He walked cautiously to the kitchen console and snapped it on. Varity popped out, an extra large portion left over from the night before. Vegie-meat steamed in multi-colored plates. The rat-smell combined with the odor of food made Pollard sick. He vomited in the sink; forced himself to calm down and made another attempt to eat something. He wasn't hungry and left most of the food in the bowl. Then he did something extremely strange and irrational. He set the bowl of leftovers in the corner near the disposal unit where he last saw the rat. He dimmed the lights and silently waited. It wasn't long before an ugly head with bristling whiskers appeared. The rat ate greedily. Its teeth flashed like deadly needles. Pollard was fascinated and frozen with emotion. When the rat finished eating, it slid like ooze back into the dark corner.

Days passed. Pollard kept feeding the rat. Pollard started eating less in order to feed the insatiable creature. He was fascinated by the beast. He almost felt sympathy for the rat that, after all, was stuck in a totally alien environment. More than anything Pollard was enjoying the surge of fear induced by the rat. It was the most horrible thing he had ever experienced. The animal stank with disease and violence. Pollard found he had less need for stimulants and he was no longer indulging in Dream Faction. He was actually living off the emotional energy provoked by being in such close proximity to the rat.

After one week, Pollard noticed some changes. The rat seemed more subdued and less frightening. The creature even let Pollard reach out and touch its' slimy skin. Pollard became even more daring with the rat in order to feel the desired state of intense fear. Finally when it seemed he couldn't provoke the animal, Pollard decided to starve it. He wanted the ugly beast to be angry because he intended to kill it. The thought of murdering the rat gave Pollard a new emotional sensation, he felt powerful. The thought of murder also frightened Pollard and he enjoyed the intensity of the new emotion. He thought constantly about blood and violent death. He no longer needed Snap Offs, Blitz Balls, or his daily regimen of Varity. The man was sustained and consumed by his own emotions. He fed the rat less and watched it become more agitated. The more the rat starved, the more alive it became with what appeared to be anger and aggression. The creature's eyes caught fire like beady, red coals. Its teeth clicked menacingly. Pollard also became more alive.

Pollard had a hammer to use on the rat. He planned to feed it for the first time in days and attack the animal while it ate. He rationalized the plan by convincing himself that the rat ate too much. Pollard was addicted to the emotional roller coaster that his plan evoked. He didn't want the new sensations to end nevertheless he was compelled to kill the rat immediately. Pollard placed a bowl of food near the disposal unit. The rat leaped on the bowl. It was big -- as if it had grown more menacing in the last few days. Fur bristled as it devoured the food. Pollard felt helpless as he let the fear engulf him. He kept telling himself that he had to kill the rat. It was a disease-ridden mutant that endangered the life of the whole city. He slowly lifted the hammer -- then quickly slammed it down. A scream echoed through the cubicle. Pollard felt sick -- the hammer missed. The rat lunged at his hand and bit down hard. A large chunk of flesh was torn away and Pollard was screaming. He could see blood and the grisly white of bone. This was the first time he ever experienced physical damage. In a disease-free society everything was safe and there were no memories of accidents. Pollard stared at his hand and fainted.

When the man woke in a pool of sweat and blood he felt changed. The rat was peacefully sleeping. Pollard felt feverish, saliva oozed from the corner of his mouth. His eyes burned like cinders. He shook off the dregs of sleep and realized he was bristling with intense, new energy. The excruciating pain in his hand merely added to the ferocity. This was the first time he was aware of himself as a creature possessing strength and power. He felt totally alive. It was morning and he wanted to wake-up the world. Slowly he rose to his feet. He looked at the sleeping rat. Instinctively he knew they were friends and he stroked the slimy fur. The rat opened its pink eyes and stared knowingly. Pollard said, "Hello my ugly friend . . . Are you ready?" The beast seemed to nod its assent. "Well, then, we shall pay a visit to our friends at Federal Docket," Pollard giggled as he gingerly scooped the rat into a plastic sack and threw it over his shoulder.

Pollard walked all the way to Federal Docket. He walked across sparkling plazas and through soft, green parks. When he arrived no one paid any attention to him. The Info-probe admitted Pollard with usual disease-free haste. Pollard released the rat in the conference hall. At first no one noticed. Soon, however, the rat made itself known by leaping and attacking, ripping and biting, tearing and devouring the flesh of dumbfounded employees. The hall echoed with screams. Pollard ran after Coleus and waved his bloody hand at her. She turned ghastly pale. Pollard grabbed her and bit her neck until blood oozed over her fleshy throat. She flailed and stammered. When he released her she fell to the floor and embraced his feet. Coleus was infatuated and infected. She never felt such extreme emotions in her life. She never felt so alive. Everyone panicked. There was violence, fear and pain. Everyone was in ecstasy.

No one was able to stop Pollard and his rat. People were overcome with exquisite, new emotions. They couldn't get enough of the terrible sensations the man and rat provided. The city of Benthos Ten awoke to a new dawn of sheer madness.

An Alien On Earth

{News Item: "UFO occupants were seen in Indiana on the 22nd of October. Mrs. Jonathan commented on the creatures, 'They looked confused. They would hop in the air. Their feet would rise up slowly and their arms would flop funny.'"}

David's world was strange. He was always on the verge of psychic vision. He lived on the border between dimensions, on the boundary between forbidden worlds and improbable realities. David saw through an invisible globe set in the middle of his forehead. Everything swarmed into his brain like warped images perceived in a fishbowl filled with a viscous fluid.

The world-city was evolving. Individuals would get lost, confronted with specters of the future and unexplained phenomenon. Strange, unknown spires appeared to rise out of the hills at twilight. Unusual buildings suddenly appeared then vanished. Whole new sections of the city were built and no one knew how or why. The landscape changed and towers shifted. New vistas were suddenly visible.

People were also changing. Unknown individuals rose to positions of power while familiar leaders disappeared. Names were changed and disguises fabricated. There was an all-out effort to draft everyone into BANS (Become A Neighborhood Spy). It was fashionable to wear gasmasks and carry digital recorders.

The towers of the surrounding city interceded with provincial bric-a-brac, pyramids, and unrelated geometries. There was a concrete sky with no clouds. City streets were devoured by Cancers, titanic corpuscles slithered through dark alleys -- machinery coughed up deadly vapors.

The eagle claw was the sign of truth. Eyes ran limp with rage and futility. The city was non-Euclidean, a magic empire of dream visages. Reason was no longer evident. Beauty meant slavery. The clockwork towers were busy churning out new phantasms.

♦♦♦ <u>Road Kill</u> ♦♦♦

The blood wouldn't upset him if he imagined it was part of an abstract painting instead of something dead. It was just a random event, but somehow it seemed relevant. Try as he might, Frank Field couldn't quite decipher what it meant or why it was so fascinating. "One moment you are walking along," he thought, "and the next, you are road kill." Was his life really that cheap? Were his experiences that random?

Frank was thirty-two, healthy, moderately successful, and deeply in love. Nothing to worry about, right? Wrong! He was dying. Everyday the realization hit him with greater certainty.

He worked with mentally ill adults and knew the danger of

identifying too much with clients. He was an Art Therapist and loved his work. He was also a professional artist, working on a series of paintings for an upcoming show, his first one-man showing in Los Angeles. His art was a mixture of styles: Realism that melted into Abstract Expressionism.

Frank came from a talented lineage. His cousin was the noted artist, Mortimer Field, who had recently disappeared from a mental hospital. Frank dreaded that ominous connection. It was difficult to separate himself from the shadows cast by Mortimer and his obsessions. He worried about the genetic predisposition to mental illness. Frank worried about the repercussions resulting from Mortimer's dubious discoveries. He was never close to his cousin; but he did receive a few messages from Mortimer, warnings really, just before he disappeared. Frank did his best to put all that aside; after all, he was in love. Andrea was his claim to the happiness he felt and just one of the reasons why he did not want to die.

"Where were you, just now," Andrea asked.

"Sorry -- just thinking." Frank shifted his concentration. She was so beautiful, he thought. She glowed even in the dim lights of the restaurant. They had been coming to this place for the last six months since they met. It was their private oasis, far away from the frenzy of upscale Los Angeles. It seemed to exist outside of time.

"I love this place," She said.

"And, I love you. I couldn't resist saying that," He laughed. They both laughed. Frank couldn't believe how good he felt.

Andrea was a mystery. Frank knew little about her. She said it didn't matter. It was their feelings for one another that mattered . . . all that mattered. He knew she was independent, probably wealthy. She never worked, lived in a fashionable condo near Westwood. Sometimes, she would go away for days at a time, there were never any explanations. But when they were together nothing else mattered, she gave herself to him completely. Frank was more than satisfied. He could never stop gazing at her as if she were some goddess with her raven hair and dark, enveloping eyes. Her pale skin appeared luminescent. Her smile evoked images of ivory, depicting immortal beauty. She had a tattoo, which seemed odd at first; but now he couldn't imagine her without it. The tattoo was a mystery in itself, depicting a cross within a maze of fire; it was placed over her heart.

♦ ♦ ♦

"Come out of it, man," A middle-aged guy with blond hair and a paunch was shaking Frank.

"What . . ." Frank stammered. He couldn't recall who the guy was. Couldn't recall anything.

"Yeah, man . . . you had too much to drink." He looked at Frank. "What's wrong . . . don't you know me?"

"I . . . can't remember."

"Hey, man . . . I'm Phil . . . compadre, you remember."

Frank didn't remember, but he decided it was better not to argue.

"Come on," Phil pulled Frank to a standing position, "Let's go for a walk. You gotta tell me everything."

"What . . . what do you want to know?"

"Frank, man . . . everything . . . about the group . . . the weapons. You went in without me, undercover. Now, man, you gotta report."

Frank didn't know what was happening or what this guy was talking about. He didn't know what to say. He was still confused, but he remembered something about one of the clients at the clinic, a patient who believed in demons.

"No. That's not it. There are no demons. There is no cult. It's the terrorists, man. The foreign bastards are fucking everything in America. We want to know about that. And the girl, Frank, what about the girl?"

Did the guy mean Andrea? He didn't want to involve Andrea.

"Frank." Now, there was a menacing edge to his voice, "don't play dumb. It's not working. The electricity didn't seem to jog your memory. But we have other methods . . . more effective methods."

Afraid to move, he finally recognized his surroundings: metal corridors without windows -- the ever-present sound of machinery -- muffled screams from behind prison doors. He recognized Phil also: the soldier with the equipment -- the man with the wire, scalpel, and blowtorch.

♦ ♦ ♦

Frank stared at Andrea, sitting across from him at a table in their favorite restaurant. Something was wrong. The lights dimmed, Andrea faded like an image on celluloid. As the darkness closed around him, Frank saw a reflection of himself in a wine glass. He was a dwarf, a wizened old man. Darkness settled with the sound of drums and whistling flutes. He saw tiny explosions, sparks; and a fire ignited in a pit at the heart of an enormous chamber. Signs, symbols of unknown origin, covered the walls like graffiti.

Frank was restrained. Ropes bit into his flesh. He was gagged so he couldn't scream. His eyes were held open with clamps. He recognized the inverted pentagram above a stone altar. He wanted to vomit to expel the rising stench. He was forced to swallow his own bile. Half-naked women and children surrounded the altar with bowed heads touching the stone floor. An imperious woman stood before the chanting crowd. A naked youth was shackled to the altar table. He looked like a statue carved from veined marble. Frank recognized Erik, a patient from the clinic, the one who believed in demons. He appeared calm, almost eager to be tortured, sacrificed. The dark Queen turned toward the altar to beckon the God of Death. Familiar sounds of machinery vibrated through the chamber as the unholy Avatar appeared with instruments of destruction.

◆ ◆ ◆

Frank had just finished a painting that depicted a grotesque chamber inside a mountain. It was part of a series of paintings about rituals. He wasn't sure where he got the ideas. Sometimes, these images seemed to be branded onto his brain, he could think of nothing else until they were committed to canvas. He considered his recent work. The paintings were strange even by his standards. People appeared to melt into disordered atoms. Huge, metal boxes floated above cauldrons of bubbling oil. Strange symbols and codes were scattered at random throughout the paintings. Frank was confused by his own creations yet he felt close to an answer, close to understanding the symbols. If he could crack the code maybe he could make sense out of the confusion his life had become. He would learn the meaning behind it all.

◆ ◆ ◆

In the dark he made love to Andrea. This was always a mysterious act without rules or boundaries. She hung above him like a pale ghost caught between life and death, moving in and out like some sea creature swimming in a forest of coral. Every touch, every sensation was heightened and expanded as their bodies connected. Frank felt the pulsing heat from a firestorm. He heard the thrum of machinery as Andrea dissolved like thin tissue on a hot grill. Frank was fucking Erik, his co-worker at the clinic, not a patient but a friend and lover. Erik moved without effort, floating like a dancer. He and Erik had been together for over six months. The boy's smooth body was tight and lean. His dark eyes conjured images of elfin creatures and lost worlds. His messed hair gave him the appearance of a wild man ready to take on any challenge, ready to experience any new thrill. Frank held onto his lover, not wanting to let go. *This is the answer*, he thought, *this is what I've always wanted. This connection, this happiness.*

◆ ◆ ◆

Frank's mind seemed to slip and he felt himself replaying the last six months of his mother's life. Everything seemed to result in sixes: 666 . . . the numbers kept repeating. They appeared in his paintings. She was diagnosed on the sixth of January, died six months later in June. She was sixty when she died. She had inoperable Cancer that devoured her, changed her from a vital, active woman into a hunched, bald caricature of herself. She had aged a hundred years. Frank remembered helping her with medication to ease the pain, but the meds were not enough. She never complained; she was the bravest person he had ever known. Right up to the end she would have her nails manicured, the last of her hair set, styled. It wasn't vanity, but a kind of pride. With all her failings, she knew she did her best and wanted that pride to show in her appearance. Before she became ill, he remembered sitting with her, watching television. They saw the planes crash into the towers and she said, "The world will never be the same." Six months later, she fell. He heard her moan and call his name. She had fallen hard in the bathroom. She said she didn't want to disturb him. She was embarrassed at being too weak to go to the bathroom without his help. So she went on her own and fell. It was February. There were several other accidents, trips in the ambulance to the emergency room. She began to deteriorate. She wanted to die at home, but a fall put her in the hospital for the last time. She was frail -- with skin like thin tissue, but she looked so peaceful resting like an angel caught in the arms of death.

The noise of gunfire -- an explosion jolted Frank from his reverie. It was difficult deciphering the sounds. Were they real or coming from the

TV in the next room? Lately, he had trouble understanding reality. Was he really an artist? Did he work at an outpatient clinic? Was there really a war going on? What happened to Andrea? Or was it Erik? He looked around the unfamiliar room. He had to squint because there was so little light. There were heavy sheets covering the windows. It was a large room, there were bodies huddled together on the cracked linoleum floor. He could smell sewage, he thought he saw rats picking through the garbage. He heard sounds reverberating in the walls.

◆ ◆ ◆

There was a party at the clinic. Frank helped the clients make decorations. He worked with people who were diagnosed with Schizophrenia or Manic-Depression. He taught them how to paint and work with crafts. Art helped people learn how to manage symptoms. Erik was an Aide and worked part-time while he attended college. He was nineteen and wanted to explore his creative abilities. He was Frank's assistant; tall, lean, and withdrawn. It took him a long time to trust another person; he found it easier to relate to mentally ill people because they seemed honest. Illness made some of the clients act-out but no one was intentionally hurtful. It took awhile before Erik could relax around Frank. He hardly talked except for "yes" or "no." But he was a hard worker, did what he was told and was good with clients. He could engage them and he was very supportive. Frank found the young man attractive, but knew little about him. Often Frank would encourage Erik to paint or draw with the patients. Erik was good. He had an instinctive understanding of design, color, and form. He was also good at interpreting client's artwork. He understood the psychology of symbolism.

It was an incident that occurred after work that brought Frank and Erik together. Frank left work early, just in time to see Erik being harassed by an older man on a motorcycle. The man had dyed hair and a potbelly. He looked mean, yelling at Erik. Frank heard part of it, "I own you, punk . . . you ain't shit!"

Frank ran over. Wearing his whites, he looked like a doctor. The thug drove off. Erik was shaking. Frank took him home, listened to his story. Erik met the guy over the Internet; now he was being blackmailed . . . forced to pose for photographs, forced to have sex. Erik wanted it to stop but the guy was powerful. He used threats and said he belonged to a cult that practiced human sacrifice. The guy had a weird tattoo, symbol of the cult: a burning cross in a spiral maze. Erik was terrified. Frank did what he could to comfort the young man. He let him move in. At first it was not sexual. Frank didn't want to scare him off; besides he wasn't certain Erik was attracted to him. It was Erik who wanted sex and initiated it three weeks after moving in. The thug didn't return. Meanwhile, Erik changed; became more assertive, began to smile more often. Sometimes he couldn't stop talking, he was excited about everything. He valued every new experience and was completely devoted to Frank.

Phil was an old soldier. Now in his sixties, he was retired, but he never stopped working. He enjoyed the odd jobs, undercover operations no one else had the stomach to perform. He worked for the clandestine government and told himself it was an act of patriotism. After all, it was guys like Phil who helped secure the homeland. He was part of a select group. He enjoyed the showmanship, the rituals, and the sacrifices. When he wasn't at work, he partook in his own brand of recreation: he loved to dominate and humiliate young men. He never told anyone about his predilections. No one asked. He never told anyone about the torture or sacrificial murders. He told himself he was a devout man, that everything he did was performed in the worship of his God. His devotion paid off because he had become a leader among his own kind. He was a leader in The Klavern of Death and he was helping to rid the world of corruption.

Phil's home was spotless, all chrome, plastic and black leather. He admired himself in the bedroom mirror. He was just what he wanted to be with his fat cock, big stomach, large arms, and dyed yellow hair. Phil loved his cock. He sat down in front of the computer screen, turned on the camera and started calling up Internet chat rooms. He enjoyed showing his belly and cock to horny "dudes." Some of the guys were actually virgins, confused about sex and very naïve. Phil liked sweet little faggots. The scenes always ended with him giving orders, he liked to make them squirm. He always worked up to his special connections, private listings in his web address book. He thought of them as his little, pussy slaves. One of his connections was Erik.

No one at work knew Erik and Frank were living together. It made their relationship more exciting . . . as if they were living in two different worlds. In one world, they were merely co-workers. In the other, they were soul mates and lovers. Erik was intrigued by Frank's paintings. They excited his imagination. Erik felt an underlying reality expressed in the art, a terrifying secret. So while he loved Frank and admired his talent, he was also repelled, frightened. Down deep he was jealous. He knew he could never compete against Frank's need to paint, his love for art. As Frank prepared for his art show, Erik was left alone more frequently. He withdrew, began to explore other interests. Frank would return home from his art studio to find Erik sitting at the computer, dressed in boxers with no shirt, his lean body glistening with perspiration. Erik would talk about weird stories he found on the Internet.

"They've invented a cow." Erik was staring at the screen, entranced. "It has no head and a glass stomach."

Frank listened quietly. It was awhile since he had an ordinary conversation with Erik.

"Yeah," the boy continued, "It's a milk and cheese machine, but it's still a living cow -- or is it a dead cow that still produces milk and cheese? I'm not sure."

Frank turned away, not certain how to respond. Weeks passed. Erik was getting despondent, reverting back to his withdrawn self. They were no longer having sex. Frank began to worry, but was distracted by preparations for his art show. Then, as quickly as it began, Erik was all right again. He had found something interesting, something he wanted to do. Frank was surprised by the sudden change. He was delighted by Erik's renewed warmth, sensuality -- his unquenchable appetite. They decided to have dinner in their favorite restaurant on the outskirts of Los Angeles, near the beach. Erik glowed with energy. They ordered wine. Frank admired the muscles that danced beneath Erik's thin, cotton shirt. Erik's black eyes admired Frank's face and torso. In an instant the mood was shattered by a gunshot. No. It was just the TV in the next room. Then they were home in Frank's bed; sated, filled with exhilaration, sexual exhaustion -- and talking as if the last few weeks never existed, confiding in one another. There was something Erik wanted to do. He

told Frank about *The Resurrection*. It was a party, a rave, and "The
Disciples of Doom" would be performing. Frank realized it was a rock
group, probably heavy metal, one of Erik's favorite bands. It wasn't
Frank's kind of music by any means, but Frank knew he had neglected
Erik lately -- he wanted to make up for it so he decided they would go to
The Resurrection.

◆ ◆ ◆

The thing in the road jerked. Frank wondered if it was an autonomic
nervous reaction or if it was still alive. He didn't want to touch it, didn't
want to find out. Suddenly he was filled with an overwhelming sense of
remorse.

◆ ◆ ◆

Frank had never been to a rave. It wasn't what he anticipated. He
expected to see lots of young adults and teens, dazed and drunk. But he
didn't expect to see so many older people or so many dressed in weird
costumes. It was held in the desert at a place called Giant Rock. In the
1950s, large gatherings were held at Giant Rock where people were
expecting flying saucers and the return of aliens. Many strange stories
were circulated about the Rock. Supposedly there were many unusual
sightings.

A large stage was set up near the Rock. Enormous puppets, twelve
feet tall, surrounded the area like centurions. Elaborate tents, like
something from an Arabian Fable, were erected around the perimeter.
The entrance to the rave was a huge, curving arch that shimmered as
people passed through, as if they passed into another dimension. It was a
great special effect. A full-scale village stood on the other side of the
arch. Frank marveled at the construction and detail. It must have been
made from papier-mâché' and Styrofoam, but it looked exactly like a
street that could exist in some Medieval City. He was amazed at the
work that had gone into creating the sets and illusions. Erik's eyes were
shinning with delight like a kid on his birthday. He looked great in his
tight, blue tank-top and low-slung jeans. He wore new, maroon boots.
Frank in his white shirt and chinos looked fussy and out-of-place, but he
felt welcome. He had no worries, didn't have to think about anything.
Music was everywhere: crashing sounds, waves of voices. All he had to
do was dance.

Drums were beating and Frank felt as though he was flying. Erik was spinning, whirling like a dervish, his eyes were flashing with the lightning cascading in huge arcs across the stage. Frank was no longer in control -- he felt the world shift. Suddenly the sky was burning. Everything appeared to melt. People became misshapen parodies of themselves. Everyone was on drugs -- shooting crystal meth -- high on **X**. Frank felt the effects burning through his brain. He wandered through the crowd feeling lost and alone, looking for Erik. He wandered into a red tent, into a frenzy of naked bodies. Some kind of beast was thrashing around in the middle of the orgy. Hands pawed at Frank's crotch. Andrea kissed him passionately, unzipped his pants. He was in the throes of ecstasy and torture, torn apart. The chamber was enormous, strange writing covered the walls like graffiti. The roar of a motorcycle hit Frank like the blast from a furnace. He turned to see the thug with yellow hair riding away from the crowd. Erik was on the back of the motorcycle. Frank called out. He stumbled toward them, but it was too late. The street erupted with gunshots, a car exploded, bodies flew apart. Frank saw the sky turn blood red. An enormous machine hovered above the desert like a metal mausoleum on a lake of fire. Angels descended bearing weapons. The dead were returning to decimate the living. It was the Resurrection.

◆ ◆ ◆

The thing in the road jerked. "Bodies are used up all the time," Frank mused, "and bodies become road kill or collateral damage." Frank was already dead. His body no longer mattered. His memory was part of a machine, part of the thrumming in the walls. A tiny spark of intelligence still existed to ruminate over the past and question the meaning of existence. Perhaps he should have taken Mortimer's warnings and crazed rants more seriously. Then again, he felt satisfied in his current state of non-existence. He would be thirty-two years old forever and would never have to worry about his body or his health. Now he would always be in love; and, more important, he would always be loved in return. Erik or Andrea no longer mattered. Only Death mattered. It was Death, the angel with the scythe, who would be his lover forever. It was Death who ruled the world.

A Cyber Report On The Brave New World

The Great Depression of the 1930s returned to devastate the planet. At the same time the dynamic expansion of the 1950s and 60s reached incredible new proportions. The conflagration of the 80s was re-ignited. Sixty-story shopping malls shot up like giant parking meters. New trinkets and gadgets flooded the streets. The Donald Duck, Godfather Clock was a hot new item. It spoke the time, sang six Italian Arias, and dispensed the 'kiss of death' to unwanted visitors.

Inflation was back like the disreputable cousin who always wants more money. High prices often necessitated a trip to the pawnshop or slave auction. People could sell themselves into slavery in order to pay off debts.

Watching Eyes

Everyone was watched. It was only proper to watch. David Oblivion's main concern: he didn't know who was watching. It could have been ordinary paparazzi, or more likely, lethal enemies. Invader spies moved in-and-out through the tv-puter-phone. He saw Johnny Carson morph into David Letterman. Martha Stewart came into his room, sat down and took notes. There was a Bush "plant" outside his window. The Synchro-mime Company wanted David's mind. He was aware of the techniques they used at the Repulsion Bureau, the CIA, and other places like Disneyland. He knew how they vacuum-cleaned a mind and turned someone into a wholesome American. He decided to ward off danger with numbers and riddles, magic words and charms. His self-deception would turn enemies into counterfeits.

The New Order

{News Item: "The Surge in Iraq is working but as many as ninety-nine people died yesterday as a result of two female suicide-bombers."}

Magnumopolus was perpetuated by Zeitgeist. It took ten thousand *flux-years* to construct. Dr. Rubin S. Andros was the scientist who programmed the Zeitgeist Mainframe.

Advertising engineers were the Holy Gurus of the age spreading the mantra, "Go and Buy."

"The purpose driven life" was one of consumption. Zeitgeist produced the products that controlled the masses.

Conspiracy, Hoax, or Alien Plot

{News Item Circa 1975: The Vietnam War continues to rage. Province after province is falling prey to the Viet Cong. President Ford and Secretary Kissinger continue to make urgent pleas to Congress for more money to reinforce the South Vietnamese Government."

News Item Circa 2007: The number of American Troops who commit suicide is six times greater now than four years ago at the start of the Iraq War.}

David knew the truth and sent an anonymous blog to the Cyber Zone where it was immediately deleted. He declared that wars were a hoax. With his Third Eye he saw the stage-sets where they were produced and enacted. To stage a war, mere acting wasn't enough. For the sake of realism wars were produced with real people, no actors and no stunt-doubles. David knew the wars were perpetrated by Hollywood and Television-City on the explicit orders from Washington. People were enlisted to be killed -- it was the most incredible waste ever conceived for the sake of public consumption.

To back up his assertions, David was obliged to list another thousand-fold-deception from the annals of American History and based on anthropological evidence: The Four Horsemen of the Apocalypse, a riveting television production that played to rave reviews for eight explosive years. "Best yet," gushed the defunct Senate Oversight Committee. "Unrivaled," was the unanimous decision of the last appointed Supreme Court. "Not since Watergate has there been this much excitement," was the enthusiastic response from the first Department of Homeland Security. Everyone in that time zone knew the Horsemen: led by Bush, orchestrated by Rove, controlled by Cheney, and enabled by Rice -- they conceived and perpetrated the War on Terror. Murder and mayhem was their signature *shtik* along with penny pinching on social services (healthcare for children was called economically irresponsible while a war in Iraq racked up billions).

The Horsemen and their political cronies called their act

Compassionate Conservatism. It proved to be great fun for millions of consumers. Part of their spectacular production was the legendary flood of New Orleans and the debacle that followed. Incredible special effects: people drowning, shootings, riots in the convention center, and fights over food. Bush, the figurehead, visited the drowned city while the band played *Hail to the Chief*. The ratings shot through the roof only to be outdone by the numbers of enthusiasts for the Iraq War and the Bush declaration, "Mission Accomplished" which plunged the world into the first one-hundred years of the Apocalypse. For David, a lost alien, it was hard to fathom so much consumer-driven stimulus in one administration. Oil companies sponsored the whole show -- they made a calculated killing as gas prices soared and green house effluvium accumulated, all of which inspired a spin-off series about the "benefits" of global warming. David realized how wrong public admiration could be as everything came to a crashing halt and eventually led to the construction of Zeitgeist.

Undo Duress

Spies were everywhere. They secretly entered David's left inner ear with laser explosives. He knew his head might suddenly detonate. He needed to erect barriers. He used alien pinking-shears to pluck spies from his ears.

"The Earth is not round!" David shouted at the approaching night. "There is no globe -- that was a cleverly devised illusion. All humankind lives on a chunk of flat rock stuffed in a canvass sack. It is a sound studio, an elaborate set. The cross-country highways are on rollers. Every place is a backdrop or hologram. It looks real because no one ever sees anything else. Humans have merely accepted what they have been told. Most of the buildings in the city are empty facades. Magnumopolus is a cardboard construction, a television fantasy.

"Then, again," the alien ruminated, "this could be an exaggeration as I am forced to tell some lies in order to confuse my enemies. I am constantly being probed under the new national security regulations. My mind has been 'tapped' so I must prevaricate in order to protect the truth."

David knew the authorities used sex-probes to get information. They used cattle-prods and water-boarding to turn people into zombies. Angels were surgically altered, changed into obsequious beasts who whimpered and lied in order to survive. The drama was televised to entertain the public with a flux of fading images and lost hopes.

◆◆◆ A Boy And His Friend ◆◆◆

When they paid any attention to him at all, they called him "kid." He said he was fifteen, but he was really twelve. He hated being a kid -- hated being small. The world made him feel like shit. He hated everything except his friend. He had one friend -- and that made his life worth living.

His real name was Anthony and he lived in an area called "Hobs Hole," a burnt crater in the middle of the city. The name Hobs was an old appellation for the devil. The hole was born the night people ignited themselves and blew up the barrio. No one knew whether it was boredom or misery that caused them to set the fires. The burnt hole became a sanctuary for mutants from the industrial hub of the city where eternal fires in the atomic power plants burned brightly.

Anthony's home was the foundation of an abandoned building. Charred concrete was covered with gunnysacks and debris to form a cave. Florescent paint was splashed on the walls. A dirty toilet sat in the center of the room like an altar stuffed with pornography. There was an overflowing sink in the corner. Several stained mattresses were strewn across the dirt-encrusted floor. An old stereo operated off a ten-volt battery, churning out rock-and-roll. A small generator supplied power to a sixteen-inch TV that constantly flickered.

Everyone called mama a "skank." Names didn't bother her. She got high on angel dust and fucked constantly. She taught Anthony several ways to be a "man." He did what he was told, but didn't think it was much fun.

Poppa wore a dress. He liked to be humiliated in front of other men. He never paid any attention to Anthony.

Big brother was a sadist. He enjoyed playing with Anthony. He wrapped the *kid* in tape and stuck him with pins. Sometimes he used Anthony like a punching bag.

Uncle loved booze. He drank rubbing alcohol when he couldn't get cheap wine. The drunker he became the more attention he paid to Anthony. He always had a hard-on for the *kid*, but Anthony never enjoyed that kind of attention.

Needless to say, Anthony spent most of his time away from home on the burning streets, in alleys and sewers. He listened to Punk Rock and tried to construct deadly weapons. He didn't know *who* he was and hated everything, but then he met his friend.

His friend was a mutant, or perhaps an alien. Most of time he was invisible, but Anthony could always see him because they were such good friends. They met in a sewer beneath a cemetery. The boy noticed a green excrescence bubbling along the wall that faded beneath a gray mist. A creature stepped out of the mist like nothing the boy had ever seen or imagined: a huge man-fish wearing the decayed parts of corpses. It smiled revealing several layers of shark teeth. The creature was slimy and bony -- it smelled pretty awful, but Anthony managed to get accustomed to the stink.

Right away, they felt they had something in common -- call it a mutual understanding -- they liked one another. From that moment, they spent lots of time together doing friendly things.

Anthony fondly recalled their first meal together. They ate the family: momma, poppa, brother, and uncle. For the most part, the meal was raw and quite bloody, but Anthony enjoyed the food almost as much as his hungry friend.

Archival Notes From The Future: Blessed Sex

1. <u>Sex Made Legal</u>

The Sex Edict of 2081 sanctified sexual behavior, but it was a ruse. Sex was not only condoned as healthy and sane -- it was obligatory.

The Edict made sex the only sanctioned ethic. Anonymous sex was encouraged and emotional relationships were considered lewd or pornographic. Individuals were viewed as objects, products to be bought, sold, and used. Reaction to the Sex Edict was immediate and pronounced. At first everyone (except teenagers) was against the authoritarian implications of forced sex. To counter the unexpected backlash, Madison Avenue was hired. The Edict was promoted and sold to the public as a new lifestyle called, "Blessed Sex," the implication being that God approved.

On television, big-busty women leisurely stripped, drank refreshing Coke and used the empty bottles as dildos. Nothing was left to the imagination. The economy boomed. New products were invented to enhance the sexual experience. There was a growing market for quack cures to relieve symptoms resulting from sexually transmitted diseases.

The most popular TV-show was, "Johnny! Fuck Her Fast!" Every week the MC was introduced by a naked octogenarian who announced, "And, here's Johnny." Giggly housewives from the Midwest sat in a row facing a line up of young, professional males. Everyone was naked, nervously fiddling with themselves. Each contestant picked a number. A wheel of fortune was spun to match pairs according to matching numbers. Once everyone was matched, the contest began.

The object of the game was to discover the couple that could fuck the longest and hardest. A hidden panel of experts determined the winning couple. Winners went on to fuck as many of the other contestants as possible resulting in some exciting sexual acrobatics. Of course not everyone enjoyed the great sexual bonanza. There were holdouts. Religious crusaders like the reanimated Billy Graham detested the new sexual license. He often decried, "Mark my words, this Blessed Sex is not heaven sent!" As a result his church was losing money and, in the end, Graham allowed the choir girls to sing topless. Spinsters and widowers became the most outspoken foe against the Sex Edict. Vigilante groups made up of old virgins burned crosses and severed sex organs.

Most people, however, were sucked into the new sex frenzy. The Psycho Sexual Wars were slow to begin. People were too caught up in the excitement and intoxication of the new craze. Teenagers humped in the streets. Many old, retired folks were revitalized after being coaxed into a casual orgy in the park.

One unlikely segment of society that expressed *moral* outrage was The Mafia. At first, they jumped on the bandwagon and organized territories in order to boost prices for sexual favors, but there was so much free sex in back alleys and on public thoroughfares they lost money. The Godfather became outraged, claiming that so much sex was not Catholic. Wherever there were people (mostly disabled seniors) who resisted the Sex Edict the Mafia Bosses were worshipped, turned into Popes and revered as Saints.

Several Evangelical Churches were losing money as born-again members were lured away by the "temptations of the devil." The churches enlisted Storm Troopers to put an end to public sex. There was violence in the streets. Police Departments had no clear directives because so many of the old vice laws remained on the books. A whole economy continued to exist which depended on vice. An officer might entrap a victim by slurping on a stiff dick or stuffing a meaty vagina. When officers were fully satisfied they rounded up their victims and sent them to jail.

Evangelical Storm Troopers marched through the streets with Tommy-guns. People complained about the wanton violence. The government refused to get involved. The public was sold Blessed Sex and now it was being denied. Citizens wanted naked "Coca-Cola" girls and "Nike" boys rollicking in the park. Religious forces wanted to shut down free sex. Some corporations wanted people to pay for every French kiss and every indiscriminate goose. Blessed Sex was government sponsored, but there was another plan afoot. No freedom could be sanctioned unless there was payback. The government had a new war to initiate to insure "peace" and boost the economy.

2. Riots And War

People became frustrated and angry due to the hypocritical infringements on Blessed Sex. The public was being salvaged to high-interest profiteers. The only way to vent growing frustration was through sex. People sought new erotic thrills, violent and frantic encounters. The Rape Riots began in 2083. Individuals refused to be docile. They rejected the newly enacted slaughter policy regarding public sex. Men and women, bisexuals and homosexuals bonded in packs and invaded the suburbs. They roamed tree-lined streets grabbing anything that walked. They broke into houses and raped anything that moved. Death squads couldn't stop the rapists. People were enraged, wanting to give pain and receive pain. They were ready for war.

The international outrage that triggered the war was "The Holy Rape of 2084." It involved a group of thirteen sex-starved nuns from the United States. The nuns were ambassadors to the Pope from the archdiocese in Des Moines, Iowa. On November 4, 2084, his Holiness was found naked and dead with a slight, toothless grin on his wizened face. His Holiness had screwed himself to death. The thirteen nuns were laughing hysterically and shamelessly dancing around the Pope. To make matters worse the nuns were using the Pope's large, gold cross as a dildo. The playful girls were swiftly carted off and scolded by Mother Superior Armarinda of Sardinia. The nuns were never allowed to return to the States. The church was rumored to have sold the thirteen girls into sexual slavery off the Port of Crisco, Spain. The United States was outraged. America wanted its nuns. November 4th was declared International Sex Day and War was declared on November 5th.

The Psycho Sexual Wars were fueled by the Holy Wars that began in Iraq. Many ideals were defended or repudiated: should society permit all sex, some sex, or no sex; is the Holy Cross really God's Penis and can it be used as a dildo -- and finally, can masturbation stunt growth or increase size? This was all part of the master plan to finalize total control in Zeitgeist. Wars have always been the answer helping to reorganize society and stimulate the economy.

III
BACK TO THE PAST

❖❖❖ <u>**The Last Party**</u> ❖❖❖

The party was unfolding smoothly, but David Oblivion's alien senses were alerted after sneaking into the bathroom for some relief. While pissing, long and golden, he stared at the figure who stared back from the mirror. He laughed at first, in amusement and amazement -- the red faced, curly-headed figure with tight pants was an obvious fake -- a drag queen, an imitation Botticelli with a powder-puff puss. The figure behind the mirror bantered and squirmed trying to impersonate David who realized the figure was a vicious agent from Zeitgeist.

Once the agent knew David was aware of his identity, he began to remove his disguise. David stared transfixed as the image in the mirror tore at the plastic copy of David's own face -- ripping out the eyes, David's *eyes*. It was so realistic that blood began to flow as he tore off rubber skin and body parts. He stood before David: a blond, slender creature vacillating between male and female freely offering his lascivious body. He giggled and leaped up-and-down pinching his breast and ass, turning into a grinning parody. He grabbed a knife and began to carve off pieces of himself, offering bloody chunks while laughing hysterically. When David reported the incident to Party Officials he could hardly contain his fear. They unwisely dismissed his concerns and told David to "chill." He was already chilled to the bone.

Warning voices drummed in David's ear, "Coppertone, Coppertone -- choosey mothers choose Jiff -- fade baby, fade!" Lyrics from a rock song constantly spoke to him, "Can you find your way or do you want my vision. In my special perception I know the right direction." The words promised rescue, but he was surrounded by darkness.

The House Next Door

{News Item: "It has been disclosed that the CIA was linked to schemes involving the assassination of rulers of various countries who professed an anti-American sentiment."}

David Oblivion's home was a typical "cell." The comrades were working for the liberation of the proletariat and the overthrow of the government.

Princess Aurora was the Chairmen of the cellblock. She managed affairs and dictated style. She always exemplified proper party behavior.

It was a matter of cell policy that no one listened to anyone. Suggestions were not followed and warnings never heeded. Each comrade had to learn self-defense because they could not be certain of anyone's real identity.

David's roommates somehow managed to give emotional support to one another while fostering their individual peculiarities.

At night when David snuck into Derek's room to peek at his pornography he saw swamp-gas rising from the vanity while iridescent lizards dashed in-and-out.

Justin Adams rode motorcycles and dismantled cars. He was very secretive and hid his life in a black bag handcuffed to his wrist. Princess Aurora burned brightly on a higher plane of reality. Sometimes she was disabled by the loneliness of the soul, but she always stumbled onwards searching for the moment of complete consummation.

David, of course, was an Alien disguised as human -- forced to alter his appearance. He foraged through Salvation Army Boxes searching for camouflage. People shuddered in amusement when they saw his disguises, but his true visage remained hidden.

Shouting, "Areba, areba," Derek jumped through the air like a bearded gazelle. Wearing a Russian Cape and fur cap he was an antic *player of games* -- flying into his harangue, poking fun and lisping laughter like a legendary bandito -- cat-calling and countering his adversaries by tickling them to death under tables and over couches. Playful tricking and bravado were part of the camouflage of disguises to counter useless information from TV. The ruse created stopgaps so the comrades could formulate strategies while David listened to God speaking over the radio (as sometimes happened in an altered state of consciousness). They all played a game, disguising themselves with hats, flounces, and berets -- vanishing within flurries of multi-colored patterns and prints to reappear in grand costumes. Winking and prancing in-and-through the clutter they would save the world by unraveling the secret of the cryptic universe. David paused to listen to God, "How's your Boogaloo?" A fading spy disguised as Shirley Temple flickered on the screen.

Back to the Party

{News Item: "A war crime of unprecedented dimension is unfolding as we avert our eyes." Robert C. Koehler}

It took weeks to prepare for the party. The roommates sent invitations on soiled toilet paper daubed with paint. On the surface they were celebrating the joys of product-oriented consumerism. In truth the comrades converged to wait for the return of Comet Kohoutek, a millennial event. They waited for a message from the stars. They had heard incredible rumors that the black, canvass sack surrounding Earth had been penetrated by an "Intelligence From Beyond."

Derek Lawless programmed the information tapes. David helped Princess Aurora with decorations. Justin Adams rummaged through back alleys and thrift stores for party disguises. The comrades displayed pictures of their favorite revolutionaries: Martha Mitchell and Jayne Mansfield. They cleverly paid homage to revered traitors like Johnny Carson in order to minimize probing suspicions. They carted crippled manikins to the house and dressed them in exotic rags. Silver Mylar was tacked to the ceiling. When they finished, the house was the perfect illusion-of-confusion to befuddle infiltrators -- a labyrinth of trash. The roommates created rooms where no rooms previously existed. They filled open space with walls. Only a true comrade could interpret the symbols to discover the truth.

Derek prepared most of the food, experimenting with recipes discovered in an ancient book of alchemy. David saw Derek holding a dead chicken and waving a plastic crucifix (this concerned him, but only momentarily). The dumbfounded alien helped prepare the Grand Punch. Derek used his electronic Pulverizer to mash solids into smelly elixirs. The drink bubbled and steamed in a swirling maze of violet hues.

Princess Aurora prepared herself in the mirror and Justin Adams ruminated in his black bag. When the comrades arrived, nothing was quite ready -- a clever diversionary tactic to keep the enemy confused. The roommates ushered each new guest into a large, dark closet where there was an enormous box of masks and disguises. Each comrade had to pick a disguise in the dark, a cautionary tactic to keep everyone's identity concealed.

Undercover Mutants

{New Item: "The offensive began with a week long aerial blitz. Medical officials reported more than 869 deaths, at least half of them civilians."}

David watched as people kept stumbling over one another, blindly groping in-and-out of rooms, corridors, blind alleys and traps set to catch undercover counter-agents. Everyone was camouflaged. A person disguised as Derek Lawless wore red hot pants, shoes embroidered with dragons, and a yellow satin shirt.

Justin Adams looked like a character from the film "Casablanca," dressed in an immaculate, white suit with a panama hat. He was pretending to be incognito behind rose-tinted glasses, but David's unearthly vision pierced the façade.

Princess Aurora imitated herself. Stunning. Her hair swirled high with spit curls framing her forehead. Blue blush by Revlon accentuated her mesmerizing eyes -- eyes that seemed to speak with a particular urgency. She wore a sleeveless, black frock that appeared formal and elegant as Aurora floated across the room. Her feet were adorned with patent leather sandals and her nails were painted platinum-green. She kissed David demurely; then disappeared into the crowd of admirers to greet fellow comrades.

David painted his face silver. He used a shiny mirror to disguise his third eye. He wore a bleached wig, erratic and frizzy. His silver pants were tucked into aluminum boots and his shirt was made from Mylar. He ruefully smiled over his clever deception: he was a real alien camouflaged as a fake.

The comrades nervously anticipated the formal initiation of proceedings. David spied the Homily Zombie trying to infiltrate. He was dressed like a nun waving a crucifix and holding a chicken under his habit. He got confused and fell through a camouflaged window. The first order of business was performed in Justin's room. It was the ritual of disoriented communion. Solemnly the honored guests passed the *spliff* from hand to mouth and on to the next. Solemnly everyone puffed, inhaled, and became silently exalted. Glittering fractals burst from dilated pupils. The tranquil whine of Jackson Browne helped unite the comrades. Holly Hock Blanchhart was writing revolutionary poetry dressed in her Chinese kimono with feathers in her hair. Anthony chanted "Hari Krishna" prayers. More people shuffled around the room wrapped in artifice and illusion that only David could penetrate with his alien eyes.

The Main Event

{News Item: "It has been confirmed and documented: torture was authorized by U.S. Government Officials."}

Comrades gathered in the central intelligence room. A few people were lost in the maze leading up to the event. Agents were already attempting to break through the cell's defenses. There was a parade of punch bowls, chip dip, and various trays of curios (comrades marching to the sea like mad-hatters and tortoises). TV monitors were turned-on as a diversionary tactic. The monitors flashed messages of complicity with the power brokers and moneyed masses, liberals and conservatives, leading everyone in unified prayer to Ford, Disney, General Electric, Las Vegas -- chop, chop -- booze, brawls, lies and the reassembled American dream-corpse. Comrades watched -- and turned up the stereo, *Rhinos, Winos, and Lunatics* spewing, "His eyes was full of wisdom but his mouth was full of shit . . ."

The radio sputtered, "Characters at the Oakdale Lounge reported seeing strange lights in the sky. My guess is that the good folks over at Oakdale have had more than enough to drink."

The business at hand was just beginning, codified as "double speak." The invading agents dripped from the TV, but they were harmless. Spies melted like globs of innocuous gas. David and his compatriots played safe and continued their counter intelligence charade. They listened to the news like every other concerned American. They were trying to discover clues and information concerning the tactics of Zeitgeist. They pretended to be dumb or simply amused, but wisely listened to the stereo, messages of revolution: The Who, Janis, and Hendrix. They listened to Rick Derringer, "Rock and roll hoochie-coo. Lawdy momma light my fuse. Rock and roll hoochie-coo. Truck on out and spread the news."

A radio announcement warbled above the music, "More rumors about UFO sightings -- Mrs. Edna Tobey, a 97 year old widow, declared the so called crafts are an advance-guard from the planet Mars."

The comrades passed joints and drank punch, pretending to get polluted, but in fact David realized everyone was becoming more attuned to one another and deciphering the dangerous messages in the media. They had pleasant tête-à-têtes pretending to be amused with trivial conversation. In fact, each gesture and every expression had a double meaning.

Princess Aurora spoke with tears about the film *Red Dust* with Jean Harlow and Clark Gable. "Such drama," she lauded, "such human pathos and romance. Real people fighting for the ultimate truth -- ruled by purely selfish emotions. Oh, love -- love and a whore!"

All the comrades in the neighborhood attended the meeting. David saw a man dressed like an extinct Tutu Bird. He listened to snatches of whispered conversations:

"There you are Fraulein Eva."

"This is . . ."

"Solo, Napoleon Solo."

"Solo, it is a curious name."

"Help! Someone -- there's a body!"

"Mr. Solo may be attractive but he is a very dangerous man, indeed." David looked, but saw no body.

Anthony sat in a corner and chanted, "Om Shanti Om." The Cosmic Lady unfolded her Tree of Life. Tristan roamed the room dressed like the "Blue Boy" by Gainsborough.

The radio interrupted David's musings, "Astronomers have focused their telescopes on a new anomaly: colored lights in the thin Martian atmosphere."

The gypsies from Church Street attended the meeting. They lived in a storefront and told fortunes. Big Mamma sat in the window and pointed at strangers, beckoning and enticing. She shared her window with plastic statues, candles and rubber Azaleas. The store was furnished with red couches, Formica tables, and three TV consoles. Each woman in the family had her own "beauty-chair" with hairdryer attached. They were the vanguard of the revolution -- always disguised, running errands, and channeling information.

The stereo played, "I want to jump, jump, jump . . . The water's cold. I want to freeze my very soul."

News alerts were broadcast, "A recent sighting of a strange explosive gas has just been observed on the surface of the planet Mars."

Everyone was acting, posing, and changing outfits. Information was dispersed, but David had a queasy feeling. He sensed secret agents stealthily infiltrating the party.

The radio warbled, "Due to mechanical difficulties our report about strange lights in the sky has been interrupted. We will return with breaking news after a short serenade of relaxing music."

Mutants With Bad Manners

Ken Strand served drinks while everyone watched "King Kong" starring Faye Wray and a giant ape. The comrades cheered the ape. David was confused. Meanwhile, Princess Aurora was having a grand champagne-coterie with Varushka who had just returned from a dangerous mission. Bubbles burst like incendiary bombs and everyone giggled hysterically.

People were dissolving before David's eyes. Mary Pickford

whimpered in a corner. He heard the frantic beating of vampire wings.

The radio belched, "A strange, metallic cylinder has landed in the vicinity of Grover's Mill . . . we now take you back to the Hotel Martinet in Brooklyn for an interlude of dance music."

People were changing. The Princess was suspicious. She took precautionary action, taking various men into the bathroom for interrogation. She was in the bathroom for hours with a big, muscular brute -- a difficult suspect. David heard strange sounds seeping through the bathroom keyhole, indecent sounds -- lip smacking. He was aware of rumors concerning water boarding, but knew the Princess would never allow torture. Finally a husky voice exclaimed, "yes, yes!" It was another successful interrogation.

The comrades were forced into a precarious position, spies had infiltrated. Everyone was a parody. The intelligence barriers were destroyed. An impromptu, incognito meeting was organized to classify new information before the comrades were completely inundated with counter agents. Someone dropped a napkin, the sign to organize. David took mental notes.

A great deal of information was assimilated. Everyone agreed the "sentinels of darkness" were present and they had to devise diversionary tactics.

A mysterious man in a robe took the initiative by dashing to the stereo to play another recorded missive. He chose *Hari Krishna Chants*. The exotic singing mystified everyone. Visions of huge, *Ratha Yatra* carts floated in David's third eye. He saw flower and paper deities slowly move through golden-filtered sunlight. Everyone was exalted. They believed the music was confusing the enemy. David felt blessed with the sound of bells and the hollow moan of a Conch Shell.

"Pack up the kids, crank up the car. Come as you like, come as you are," blurted a mysterious voice from the TV. The comrades had been deceived!

The radio blurted more frightening news, "This is Carl Phillips at Welmett Farm in Grover's Mill. I've never seen anything like it. A thing came from the sky. It is standing in front of me, half buried in dirt."

The enemy had invaded. David was witness. Justin was hiding.

Princess Aurora locked herself in the bathroom.

David felt relief when Derek Lawless launched an alternate plan of defense. He leaped to the stereo and bravely replaced Krishna with the Rolling Stones. It looked like a brilliant deception. The Stones screamed, "I know its only rock and roll but I like it -- like it -- yes I do." The jagged screams and repulsive drumming worked like incisors to assail the lurking enemy. Everyone danced anew -- pounding and yelling and tearing at each other's disguises. The sounds were an ecstatic irritant. Next, *The Brontosaurus Stomp* pitched everyone into a frenzied oblivion. Eyes blazed scarlet as comrades tore clothes to shreds, thumping naked to the Ojays, "They smile in your face, all the time they wanna take your place, the back stabbers."

Suddenly David's acute senses were agitated. Was it a miscalculation or a counterattack when someone put Bowie on the machine, "We got five years, stuck on my eyes. We got five days, what a surprise. We got five hours -- my brain hurts a lot. We got five minutes -- that's all we've got!" Everyone shuddered.

The radio retched, "This is unbelievable. The top is moving, coming off. Something is writhing out of the shadow like a gray snake."

Everyone froze when they heard the alarm ring. Derek sacrificed himself and descended to the dark door to face the hostile invader. It was Mrs. Homily with her chicken and cross. She clucked at Derek, "Naked -- not nice -- bad manners -- too much noise!" The inscrutable Mrs. Homily walked into the living room and dissolved into Lillian, David's earth mother. She stared in disbelief, "You're a disgrace! Get dressed!"

David stood his ground, no longer human, but alien. He stared Lillian down with his third eye. She froze in mid sentence, collected her composure and ran from the room yelling, "Bad manners, bad manners!"

Information Overload

The invaders were defeated, but the party wasn't over. David wondered what happened to Kohoutek. Music was playing while people searched for new disguises. Suddenly the room seemed darker and David recognized many strange, but familiar faces. His alien vision was boosted by a shift in the time-space continuum. He saw the "pipe," the "brush," and the "bra" peeking around corners and compiling innumerable lists. Ma and Pa Kettle were having sex in a dim corridor. Marilyn brushed past throwing kisses. Mickey Mouse was chasing Kate Smith from room to room, bed to bed. The mouse had an enormous hard-on. Barry White and "Love Unlimited" panted over the stereo speakers and the air felt cloying and humid. Heartbeats conjured the sounds of "Pink Floyd" recreating a prehistoric world of insatiable heat and screaming dinosaurs.

People melted before David's eyes. Hands, feet, bellies and buttocks dripped into an ecstatic flow of carnal urgency. Everyone dissolved and began to ooze into one another. David's hands couldn't stop and he blistered with alien viscosity that was like an overload of sexual intensity. He became an enormous erection in a jungle of holes and stoppers, plugged and plugging -- feeling anonymous hot-flesh tremble beneath his trembling appendages. Light eclipsed. Sounds blurred.

"I wonder, is anybody here; or is this my private dream?" The stereo wailed. David pumped his gigantic dick in fear -- holes, stoppers, plungers, plumbers, breasts, buttocks, cocks, cunts. He felt lost. Liz Taylors creamed into Buster Crabs and dripped into Jane Fondas; slipped into Paul Newmans, Marlon Brandos, Sal Mineos, Myrna Loys -- and everybody flowed into him and he flowed back.

"It's such a scary, scary, scary dream," Rick Derringer warbled from the stereo in David's head. He prayed. He forgot where he began and where he left off, forgot *who* he was supposed to be -- forgot the code and the words.

The radio whispered ominously, "Ladies and gentlemen, I have an incredible announcement to make: capsules are landing all over the country. We are witnessing the advancing vanguard of an invading army from Mars!"

The comrades had been deceived, again. The enemy did not retreat, but advanced. O-zone agents and Time-lapse spies dropped from the sky and surrounded the house. They would destroy everything. Metallic pie-plates were landing in the living room. Hatches were opening. Grey, snake-like creatures were slithering toward David. Saliva dripped from sunken mouth-holes and they had no eyes. Each one carried a cross and dead chicken. "What happened?" David mumbled, "What happened to

Kohoutek?"

♦♦♦ <u>Story of Sam</u> ♦♦♦

"Never -- never again!" Sam Breckman muttered to himself. He was complaining about riding the bus. His old Plymouth broke down for the third time in two months so he sat in the crowded bus as it drove past the Sugar Broiler, Shabbazz Sandwich Shop, and Muhammad Temple Number Nine. He had no choice if he wanted to keep his job.

The electric bus rattled and swayed. It was packed with school kids and morning commuters. Everyone pushed. Sam had to stand. He was fifty-seven, an immigrant from Russia. He clasped the handrail for dear life and stared at the other passengers through horn-rimmed glasses. He wore an old fashioned, brown suit.

Sam was a watch repairman. He worked at Redlick's Department Store for the last six years. At one time, he owned his own shop, but there was never enough business. Sam had a wife and five *kinder*. The youngest still slept at home, but Sam was never sure what the boy did during the day -- he was nineteen now. The others were busy leading their own lives. They rarely called.

Several kids were talking loud and trashing people on the bus. They were pointing at a hippie with long hair -- called him "faggot." Sam muttered, "what do they know . . . any of them. Just kids. It isn't easy to be anyone. Life works you into the ground."

In Russia, Sam was a tailor. He designed hats for the wives of powerful party leaders. He was paid well, but circumstances changed and he was drafted. As a Jew in the Soviet Army, life was intolerable. Sam escaped to America. He was introduced to the "land of the free" at Ellis Island. The immigrants were herded through metal gates, names were shortened and recorded; some people were not allowed to leave the island. Sam had a cousin in California who could provide employment that was necessary to enter the country. The first day in New York City, Sam was called a "kike."

Once he arrived in California his cousin became his employer. He took Sam under his wing, but paid him as little as possible. Sam could no longer design hats, styles were changing and hats were old fashioned; besides, cousin Josef owned a watch business.

"How did all this happen?" The same question plagued him like a dog chasing its tail, round and round his mind, "I don't blame Josef. He taught me a skill. He said America runs on watches. When I open my own store -- business goes *kaput*. It's the damn cheap watches. I work like a dog for pennies. The wife nags. My kids -- I no longer know them! When I made hats it was better."

At the next stop, someone was helped onto the bus. Sam averted his eyes -- the man was disgusting. He had long, matted hair, ripped clothes, and strings of saliva stuck to his lips. He could barely walk, but jerked and hobbled like a drunk until he stood next to Sam. He made "mooing" sounds. Sam thought he was deaf and dumb as well as crippled.

The bus lurched forward and Sam was forced to help the broken man to his feet and hold him so he wouldn't topple and bash his head. Sam glanced at his face -- he saw a distorted mask with large eyes that leered defiantly. Finally some seats were vacated. Sam pushed the man into a seat. He was about to move away, but the cripple held on. Sam reluctantly sat down. The man moved his thick tongue and spit the words, "heyzoos, heyzoos" as his hand convulsed and jerked.

The bus turned down Sixteenth Street. Sam concluded the man was Mexican. He disliked Mexicans, but something about this man gnawed like a wound that wouldn't heal -- something besides his degenerate condition. It was the eyes he realized and risked a quick glance at the man's face. Sam was startled -- such eyes on the face of a simpleton -- eyes that possessed intelligence, wisdom not defiance. Sam was dumbfounded. He continued to peer into those perfect eyes. The bus jerked forward causing the feeble man to tumble into Sam's lap. Something changed as he cradled the other man's head. He felt old and vulnerable. His life seemed meaningless, but now he'd been given a chance for something more . . . he could help this man.

Sam surprised himself as the words tumbled from his mouth. "Come, please come to my house . . . for a meal."

The man jerked in a way to indicate a negative reply.

"What can I do?" Sam murmured.

He heard a voice in his mind, "you will follow me."

"Would you want me?"

There was no need for an answer. For the first time in his life, Sam

Breckman was truly grateful. The Messiah had finally arrived.

Party Crashers

Everyone dissolved. Comrades disappeared. The invading creatures slithered through the darkness looking for victims -- to rob them, to pickle each person's psyche in a flask of formaldehyde. Although he was confused, David knew he had to escape, to flee with what remained of his battered alien-self. He recited ancient recipes of magic. He relied on a secret book of incantations and performed rituals while speaking in tongues. His third eye glowed. He flayed his body with a spiked belt and set his faux hair on fire. Powerful words fell from his lips, but the enemy continued to advance.

Loud speakers boomed, "The house is surrounded. You have three minutes to surrender." Everything became numbers, minutes, riddles and chants. Finally, he perceived a slight shift or quake in perception. He was getting close so he waved his arms ten times and shouted blasphemous names, "Shell, Chevron, ITT, Exon -- Nikon, Nixon -- holy, holy Ford." He pinned his most potent charm in the middle of his chest and it glowed like a magic escutcheon with the all powerful invocation, "WIN." It worked. He was free. Free and fleeing.

The Old West Gambit

Before David could leave the churning inferno Big Mamma read his destiny in the Tarot Cards. He picked "Aleph," the Fool. She surmised it was a good omen, a sign of strength. It also indicated unexpected occurrences. The gypsy took his money, smiled and then turned into a magnificent, white mare. "Hop on," the horse whinnied. David quickly finished putting on his make-up and new disguise. He was leaving the debacle dressed as a rhinestone cowboy, "Have gun will travel." He became David Oblivion in the old west, an agent of justice with a license to kill. His WIN charm glowed in the center of a sheriff's badge. David leaped on the white mare and rode off into the distance.

He rode through the outlands. The world was dark, a desert with purple cliffs on the horizon. Occasionally David passed splintered outgrowths, wooden caves that sheltered lifeless shadows.

He was a bounty hunter. He saw the eyes of the man he hated (needed) on an FBI poster in the Post Office -- or, was he really staring in the mirror on his bedroom wall? The man was wanted dead or alive. He was the object of David's hatred. He stole David's rightful position in life. He was respected and honored while David had nothing. It was payback time.

That's when David's reverie dissolved. His horse turned into a cat named Gypsy and his trip into the old west was a typical night cruising for information, searching for the Underbelly -- looking for an escape clause. He suffered a close call at the party. David's extraterrestrial genesis was almost robbed and exploited. No doubt, he was severely damaged by the incestuous probes and propositions. He was confused, but he managed to survive.

Notes From The Archives: The New Economy

1. <u>Sex Commodities</u>

The Free Sex Zones of the city offered any enhancement, pain or pleasure for the asking price. Sex-organ transplants were always a hot "pop!" item, hawked from wagons for cheap street-prices or in top-notch clinics where safety was guaranteed for top dollar. Some men desired vaginas for self-insertion. People often purchased two sets of genitals for long workouts.

High fashion often resulted in the same face-and-body on all the beautiful people in the city that spawned a reaction by individuals who wanted to be different, pacesetters who wanted to look unusual. Individualists began to adopt body parts from other animals. The horse dork was always a popular item. To be different some individuals coveted what was considered ugly or disgusting. A perfect female might deeply desire an encounter with a malformed giant. Athletic, young men paid to be reconstituted as decrepit lechers or as terrifying beasts.

Most people couldn't afford proper surgical transplants and they were forced to get what they desired from coin-operated machines. Every enhancement conceivable including Wonder Beauty-Kits was sold in Splend-O-Rama automats. Playtex was the largest manufacturer of living organs. New-and-alive girdles, bras, and gloves actually formed a bond and molded the body like putty. Flab was turned into fabulous curves. Living-gloves worked like an extra pair of hands. Dispensers also carried a diverse array of physical deformities for the more discriminating pace setters.

A sign on every automat warned customers that no one could be held responsible for mal-adaptations. Organs were sealed in genetic hybrid-jelly, but there were no guarantees. All customers were advised to consult with professional surgeons before making a purchase; however, people used the machines because they couldn't afford professionals so the warnings generally went unheeded. People felt compelled to preserve or obtain sexual beauty in spite of the risks. Rumors abounded about botched machine-transplants resulting in paralysis. Surgical tools were provided with all Wonder Kits, but anxious customers often made improper incisions resulting in the loss of blood or death. On rare occasions when transplants were successful the results were truly miraculous which explained why so many people became addicted to the machines, endlessly searching for the perfect transformations

2. The Mafia Reborn

The Mafia Bosses quickly discovered that being "holy" or moral was not a very lucrative proposition so they took up their old practices with the help of quasi government-officials who forced them to pay for their privilege to extort.

IV
MAGNUMOPOLUS – CITY OUTSIDE OF TIME

At last, there was peace -- a state of affairs brought about by constant war. The city was especially dangerous. War zones shifted from hour to hour. The world was fighting the Psycho Sexual Wars of 2084. Dr. Rubin S. Andros defined the rules in his seminal book _The Guide to All Natural Phenomena_ where he stated, "War is the behavioral basis for every manifestation of life." The good doctor asserted that war equals life (war = life). Zeitgeist, the world brain, was built to maintain peace by fomenting war.

Dangerous Liaisons

David woke in the midst of the city. He wore a new disguise that consisted of a large coat and baggy overalls. A floppy hat covered his head and dark glasses camouflaged his eyes. He carried a weapon that was disguised as a plumber's plunger -- part of his new undercover identity. David looked and felt like he just crawled from a sewer. His WIN charm was pinned to his coat. He had to make an information-drop at the customary spot, but the spot changed locations as a precautionary measure. He needed to comb the city with the expertise of a secret agent to find the new location. He remained true to his name, David Oblivion.

MAGNUMOPOLUS

CITY OUTSIDE OF TIME

David Oblivion: alien-spy seeking privy information and perpetrating diversionary collusion. His gypsy cat dipped into the shadows, off on her own mission of intelligence. He felt abandoned and vulnerable so he tried meditating to regain his composure -- nothing worked.

The city was haunted -- always Halloween. Lob-eyed fiends pursued David. Drug addicts, housewives and vice-cops lingered in dark doorways ever ready to confiscate David's secrets. He walked through North Beach and observed large insects disguised as tourists stealthily snatching bits-and-pieces of the street-scene to take to their suburban ant-hills and devour.

He saw the world through an alien sensor, a third-eye fishbowl. He needed to locate his counterpart who broke away after he landed on this planet. David believed the Underbelly could help. Without his "split-half" there was no way to escape.

The city was ubiquitous, surrounding everyone in a cocoon of artificial daylight. Amusement Centers and Fascination Parlors stood in line on Market Street. Cheap clothes-stores and appliance wholesalers competed for the attention of pedestrians. Movie palaces turning to dust glittered in the sunset: "The Strand," "The Fox," "The Olympus," and more enticing names faded into the past.

On Hollywood Blvd, stars were engraved in golden sidewalks. In front of Grumman's Chinese there were hands cast in cement. The Gold Cup coffee shop was always packed with lingering ghosts who couldn't escape. The street was a replica built by Disney, extolling a rumored glory that never existed. It hadn't changed in a thousand years. Only the bodies changed, old eyes were replaced with younger, hungrier eyes. Chrome Jaguars whizzed by on a track, same cars; round and round. Parasites clung to lampposts assessing, calculating, seeking victims. Everywhere David saw casualties of the Psycho Sexual Wars.

Everyone was waiting to be discovered or sold. Hypnotic music whispered to strangers from black-holes. People disappeared into large, concrete department stores -- no one came back out. There were recent fires, burning infernos, people trapped inside.

Hustlers wandered back and forth, young country boys from the Midwest with freckles and sunburnt hair. Some wore "show all" fashions with holes to reveal the crack of an ass or the tip of a cock. Some were innocent males who hadn't started to use make-up or genetic enhancements. Hustling had become more difficult now that there was so much free sex. Usually "johns" would only pay for something special like "innocence." A hustler's naiveté and youth quickly diminished. They became sexual targets and objects of abuse. The city took its toll and hustlers became old and wasted by age twenty-three, often becoming addicts.

Sex addicts with heavy habits were called "shmeckers." The dealers kept lists of starved shmeckers and old hustlers. There was a big business selling old hustlers to one another to increase profit margins. Dealers also sold "venel" drugs that stimulated prolonged orgasms. The drugs were very addictive. A venel addict lasted three years and died in the throes of orgasm. His whole body exploded through his penis and he was turned inside out.

Sex starved hustlers lingered on street corners or in bathrooms waiting for any kind of action. A hustler's handsome face would fall in upon itself; eyes became holes of desperate yearning. David saw young bodies tremble in torment for a sex fix. Anything would satisfy: a cock, dildo, ass hole, vagina, broomstick, bottle -- anything as long as some stranger administered it. He saw muscular bodies wither into flaccid sacks of abused flesh. He saw a bloated erection on walking-death.

Mek

Mechanical surrogates and pornography were produced in "Mek Zones" where sex was rigidly restricted to the use of machines. For their own economic benefit people were urged to avoid one another. The machine was the only focus for sexual adoration and love.

♦♦♦ Perfect Love ♦♦♦

Young Billy loved his Mek Machine, Model 2000. Billy stood naked in the warm, awesome light that radiated from the machine's face. He was a handsome lad with a well-endowed body. His Mek lover was huge. Model 2000 looked like an enormous automobile carburetor with a wide, cylindrical air-filter for a head. It had innumerable coils and armatures, pipes and valves, and an abundance of plungers and stoppers.

A puffy pneumatic-mattress floated in front of a large, rubbery slit in the face of the machine. A round hologram-monitor peered down like an all-seeing eye.

Billy hopped onto the mattress. The machine hummed and chortled in a sonorous voice, "Hi, Billy -- want to diddle me?" Billy lay on his back and stared into the eye of his lover. Electric stimulators slid out from the bowels of the Mek Machine and attached themselves to various erogenous zones on Billy's body. Tiny electric shocks encouraged Billy's sexual excitement. Hot, oral sponges caressed his flesh. The porno monitor came alive with 3-D movies. Billy was very aroused.

He was watching his favorite, most exciting, diddle film, "Mek Machine Orgy," starring Model 2000, Model 1500-A, Model 700-AB, and Model 750-AA. "Ooh," Billy sighed as the machines embraced and disclosed tense cervix membranes and hard-on plunger rams. Billy's organ was very hard. He activated the "dirty-talk" soundtrack and the "rough foreplay" program. His lover clicked into mechanical action, "Hi there, Billy boy -- so, you've been diddling again. You can't hide it from me!"

Billy was about to explode. His was going out of his mind with electric shocks, porno flicks, dirty talk, and hot sponges. He wanted to masturbate. As soon as he touched himself, a metallic coil retrieved his hand and clamped it to the mattress frame. "None of that, you nasty boy -- I'll have to teach you a lesson!" Billy's legs were lifted in the air and a wood paddle smacked his upended rear-end. The young man gasped with pain and pleasure. "Now, Billy boy," The Mek lover chortled in a synthesized computer-voice, "I've got some medicine for you!" A ramrod with a nozzle danced like a snake near Billy's face. The boy obediently opened his mouth. The ram squirted jets of sex-juice into Billy's throat. It was a hallucinogen, an aphrodisiac -- and Billy loved it.

The Mek 2000 shifted gears from foreplay to heavy lovemaking, "Kachunk!" The young man sucked, "Umm, umm." The machine replied, "Ugha, ugha." Another ramrod unraveled from the machine's belly. A flexuous-tongue massaged and licked Billy's private parts. A wrap-around squeegee made messy sounds as it sucked and sloshed. A penetrating plunger titillated Billy's prostrate gland. "Ooh, ooh," Billy screamed. "Ugha, ugha," Mek 2000 replied. Another hose unraveled like a giant python -- the vacuum-suck, rubber-lips attachment wrapped around Billy's hard cock and slurped.

Billy was about to explode. The Mek 2000 subdued the boy's sexual urgency with an electric shock. "Oh Billy," the machine moaned in a fabricated voice with clacks and clicks, "Billy (click, click) my big, beautiful lover (clack, clack) -- you just got to diddle me (click, click, click); oh, I want it so bad (clack)!"

The boy lay flat on the cot and moaned in delirious expectation. Slowly, the mattress plunged Billy into the giant, vaginal slit in the face of the machine. Billy, with every orifice plugged, slid into the enormous sexual-vortex of his perfect lover. Screams merged and shattered in eerie cacophony as Billy slipped forever into eternal sexual ecstasy.

Aliens in the City

Earth's axis was shifting resulting in confusion. No one remembered why the wars were waged, but everyone knew the enemy: evolutionary beings, nature's defense against the Psycho Sexual Wars -- true androgens who stepped beyond humanity's prisons. They were not genetic freaks concocted in laboratories or synthetic, grease-paint dolls -- they were naturally evolved, diaphanous angels. They called themselves No-man, known as "Numan." They were intermediaries between any "outside" influences and humanity. David Oblivion sought their help. They were the only link to the Underbelly and they were waiting to receive his information.

The shifting of the axis produced a flux of overlapping time zones. Every moment merged -- each day crashed into the next. People floated aimlessly without knowing the correct time or century. Some people wore costumes from another era and practiced outdated customs. Every century was cogent. Pharaohs, queens, cavemen and spacemen coexisted at the same time. David was *alien* -- able to perceive the confusion of centuries.

The moat before the stunned alien was filled with giant saurian and meat-eaters that protected the inner sectors against invaders during a siege. David crossed the drawbridge with intrepid haste and entered the Free Sex Sector: Atlan, Fun City, Manhattan, Toledo. He was meticulously dressed. His hair was washed-out blonde, eyes blue behind dark glasses, and his lips were cherry red. His WIN charm glowed and he carried his trusty plunger. David missed his gypsy cat -- he felt queasy with trepidation.

Celebration in the Free Sex Sector

The alien sat on a parapet overlooking downtown. Everyone was celebrating the American Millennium. The scene was dominated by an outpouring of red, white, and blue hysteria. Stars and stripes covered tattooed buttocks and chests. Some celebrants had eagle heads that were genetically transplanted onto their bodies. Brass bands played patriotic songs. Colorful dioramas portrayed scenes of rape and pillage from the glorious past which encouraged enthusiastic audience participation. The slogan was, "Violence is peace -- aggression is abundance" taken from the best selling monograph entitled, *The Instinct for Mass Violence and the Right to Exploit*, written by The New Committee for Responsive Social Action.

A red man with white stars smashed the window of a parked car. He opened the door, jumped in and drove up Powell Street. A small crowd of stars-and-stripers cheered the man as he plowed into a lamppost. Someone tossed a lit cigarette and the smashed car became a glittering blast furnace. Excitement bristled on every city street. David studied the faces of the jubilant crowd looking for a contact (an angel). The faces appeared reptilian, infused with wanton lust.

More Sex and Frenzy

David spotted a boy on the corner. He looked like a new hustler -- blue eyes wide open with amazement as he looked around. Black curls framed his smooth face. His hard body bulged in tight jeans and his open shirt revealed a well-defined chest. The quiet alien felt the familiar gnawing ache to garner information from the young man, but he merely stared. The boy was not a friend or an enemy, just a stranger.

A large, blue woman with white stripes grabbed the boy. "How 'bout a little action, pecker boy," she hissed through green, enamel teeth. She wore an American Flag mini-skirt with chartreuse tail-feathers. Her black patent, hip boots had twelve-inch heels. Her face was covered with red-slash paint and platinum knives dangled from her ears. Her fingers were tipped with hypodermic needles filled with a vicious selection of psychedelic stimulants.

She grabbed the boy with her large hands and shoved him to his knees forcing his head under her skirt, "kid, I want you to meet Ruby the Clit -- take a nice long lick!" He struggled uselessly. Blue lady unraveled a mean, black belt, "Whacko!" The boy yelled. Lady ordered, "Eat my sweet pie -- you damn queer!" Boy's head obediently bobbed under the American Flag. "Um, um, um," Blue lady sighed, "Have I got a nice surprise for you!" She jerked boy to feet and tore his clothes off. Boy trembled. Blue lady snatched her giant, power-ram, star-studded dildo and licked the tip.

Fear registered in boy's eyes as he arched his body against the building for protection, muscles heaved and rippled. His cock jerked like a handle on a slot machine. Blue lady licked tip and bent boy in half. Two sex starved shmeckers stood nearby and jerked off. One drooling shmecker put his scabby hand on the boy's ass. Blue lady whacked him in the head, "Hands off you 'syph' creep!" The shmecker spewed vomit.

Blue lady strapped on the power-ram. Boy was bent -- his ass prone. Lady parted the cheeks with large, gloved hands, "Um, what a nice virgin hole." She drove star-studded dildo into ass. Boy screamed. She drove. "Umpa, umpa." Boy jism spattered the wall of the Mutual Life Insurance Company.

Shmeckers drooled and fingered each other. They were hobbling around Blue lady and boy, pumping enormous cocks covered with venel sores. "Umpa, umpa." Blood dripped from boy's ass. Blue lady convulsed -- juices dribbled down her legs -- she retrieved dildo and stomped down the street. Boy keeled over on sidewalk. He was pumping another erection. Shmeckers crawled over boy. Syph-sores popped. Shmeckers touched, licked, sucked, fucked, jerked-off on boy. "Gasp, gasp," boy choked. He was no longer hot, young trade. He was hooked. He was crap. Jubilant crowds passed by. No one noticed accept David Oblivion. Everyone else was celebrating.

Night descended like a backdrop in a play. City night was a glitter of ozone and flashing lights. Teenage gangs searched for victims. Addicts sought protection and a fix. Hustlers and prostitutes *turned on* to take the edge off before they faced the streets. Drag queens devoured the secrets of eternal beauty. Old people lined up to buy the latest youth enhancers. Young people reconstituted themselves with genetic replacements. Dealers worked. Pentagon officials made plans for war. Everyone sought sex. The alien was looking for a Numan, an angel.

Alien Encounters and Other Worlds

His search continued across deserted beaches through abandoned cities and condemned amusement parks; in drunk-alleys ruled by faceless overlords, above shadow-pits controlled by corporate pismires who decided which wars to prolong and which sectors to annihilate.

Danger was his business, part of being a secret, alien spy. It was imperative to keep his mind finely tuned. Often David felt considerably muddled. How could he decipher the world? How would he discover the drop-spot where he was destined to meet his connection to the Underbelly? Theoretically David had information to exchange with the proper individual. He had to find an angel (his counterpart?). The conjectures were coded, but David no longer had the key.

He sought a bar where he could dull his mind -- blur disturbing memories. The Mindshaft was a tunnel filled with art-deco lamps and mahogany furniture. Colored discs whirled round the room to the percussive beats of rock and roll. David stepped up to the bar and ordered a beer with a shot. He was surrounded by men -- looking for a contact. His alien senses were very acute. He could see everyone at a glance and understand every facial expression, every sly wink. There were no comrades -- no one even knew David Oblivion existed.

He melted into the wall -- the awareness of mild intoxication replaced by disorientation. He was no longer in the bar, but surrounded by transparent corridors of luminous fiber -- indescribable color -- floating in a sheath of unformulated energy and unlimited potential. His vision expanded -- revealing a landscape of crystal towers on a maroon horizon. The glowing pinnacles collected solar winds. This place was a living catalyst, an engram of the future. He was not alone. He was in the presence of Avatars. One danced within orbs of luminous green (the softest, lightest presence of green he'd ever known). The One who danced was his counterpart. They were bound together by destiny.

"Scuse me!" rudely raked across David's brain, "You were in my way!"

His pant leg was wet, smelled like booze. David looked in the face of a smirking denizen dressed as a fashionable Gatsby in a silver suit who looked eerily familiar. He felt like cracking his smooth smile, but just walked away into the night.

The Urban Circus

The street was a strobe -- too bright. People moved like images in an old movie. Walls glowed unnaturally, graffiti was scrawled everywhere like hieroglyphics. Every pavement was a slab of cuneiform, cleverly coded information (agent communication): "Fuck the world -- we are the sons of 2084 -- I want to be your toilet -- nowhere to run, nowhere to hide -- use me like a dog -- no virgins, no more -- the hole gets bigger all the time."

Code constantly changed -- evolving and becoming more complicated and deceptive. Often intriguing pictures accompanied the words. Whenever possible, David read the walls to discover the latest plans and most recent instructions.

A young couple was making love on the concrete plaza across the street. The crowd avoided the couple. They were softly caressing and kissing, glistening in the lights reflected off the buildings like copper figurines animated by the memory of a melody played by a music box.

Whistles and horns blared an assault on the lovers. Himmler's "Lebensraum" marched upon the scene to make a flash sex-arrest. Legality had nothing to do with excitement. The crowd had to be entertained. When the coffers were low, arrests were made to stimulate the economy.

Himmler was a *simulant*, reconstituted by Zeitgeist. The Lebensraum was Himmler's personal sex-squad, a group of males who were conceived and bred to be racially superior, Aryan Supermen. As commander of the Lebensraum, Himmler was the master-of-ceremonies for all mass arrests. He nourished the crowd's pervasive and uncontrollable instinct for violence and (as the media reported) the whole city profited.

David's alien brain collected details that could be submitted to some supreme judge who might end the atrocities -- an idle dream at best. He watched troops march forward to separate the lovers. Helicopters swarmed overhead like locusts drawing attention to the arrest. Loudspeakers were set up in the plaza. The patrol of thirty guards were dressed in ceremonial uniforms: red, metal-mesh tunics worn over blue, leather pants -- leather gloves, blue hip-boots and crash helmets adorned with white stars.

Himmler was an ageless, mammoth man with dyed, blond hair -- impeccably dressed in red satin. He announced the arrest to be part of the gala festivities planned for the American Millennium celebration. Stirring music was broadcast over the speakers: hymns, anthems, motets and synthesized Wagner. Spotlights were ignited. Display racks set up. A camera crew zoomed in for the action. The crowd gathered. The lovers were tied to separate racks. The petite, copper girl was manacled, her legs spread and her tiny breasts pointed toward the sky. The muscular, young man was tied in a spread-eagle position. The racks were metal constructions that could swing and pivot in any direction.

Himmler himself pried open the girl's vagina and inserted a mangy "Jagg-lizard." The Jagg was a parasite with bulging eyes, pincers and four rows of cannibal teeth, specifically designed and genetically produced to live on the juices and membranes of human sex organs. The girl screamed as the lizard bit. Music built to a gushing crescendo. The crowd cheered and Herr Himmler graciously took his bow. David wanted to turn away but he was frozen in place by the grotesquerie before him.

The rest of the troops were playing with the young, naked man, experimenting with whips, hot wax and burning cigarettes. The Lebensraum soldiers were agitated and excited by the sobs of their prisoner. They tried to hide their bulging erections by rubbing against a nearby building only to become more excited and uncontrollable. Several troopers knelt before their prisoner, quibbling over the possession of his beautiful penis, licking and sucking like starved dogs. Other Lebensraum were tearing at their uniforms and pulling at their own rigid endowments.

Himmler was naked -- chasing little girls. The storm troopers were throwing people on the ground and using them like punching bags.

Some troopers were fucking each other with Billy-clubs. Spotlights were overturned setting fires. Helicopters were dropping gas grenades to disperse the crowds. Everyone was screaming. People were frantic, naked and bloody. David heard Himmler's voice reverberating over the loudspeakers, "Thank you ladies and gentlemen, this event has been an overwhelming success!"

Contact

While trying to escape, the stunned alien was accosted by a sallow-faced man with a manic gleam in his eye. "Hey man," he exploded, "give me my plunger before I crack your head." Gas grenades were blasting open, panic was everywhere and here was this guy who wanted to break David's skull.

"Are you deaf," he yelled over the sound of exploding shrapnel, "I'm tired of cleaning my toilet with *White Lightning, White Tornado,* and *Mr. Clean.* I want my plunger."

David thought the guy must be insane. He held his breath. A firebomb burst.

"Look man -- someone stole my plunger and you're the only person I see with a plunger. Don't you think it's a little funny walkin' around with a plunger? You got to be *the man.*"

"But," David hesitantly replied, "It's attached."

"What's attached?"

"The plunger -- its part of me like a graft, connected with an umbilical cord." The remark was part of his cover story, a secret code.

"You got to be crazy," his expression changed and he seemed to calm down, "we can help each other. Seems we both have some information." Relief rushed over David like a warm stream. "That's right, we're working for one another. I was just checkin' you out. You must be my contact. I'm Aremet Yashafats."

"You had me going. I'm glad to meet you!" The alien said with conviction.

"This place is crazy, man. Every one of those bloody bastards -- everyone is out to get your ass. They want to hang you by the balls. No joke. Listen to me and get out. The church, man -- get to the church! You should be safer. I'll meet up in a couple hours in old-town L.A. at the art museum. Chow, man -- and good luck."

A Church Where Everyone is Welcome

David didn't know which church Yashafats meant so he sought sanctuary in the neo-gothic shrine on the far side of the plaza.

"Kyrie, Gloria, Sanctus, Benedictus."

He took a seat at the back of a rectangular auditorium and listened to hymns sung by an invisible choir, "I only know hell is getting hotter and the devils getting smarter all the time. Hallowed be my name. Have no doubts before me. I'm the Light. Hallowed be my name."

His mind seemed to be playing tricks. It was difficult to discern reality. He was in a family church, but since there were no longer any ordinary families, David assumed this was a "mock-family" church. People sat and prayed together in traditional groups: mother, father, and two children. They wore costumes: suits and ties, flower hats with skirts reproduced from a 1955 *Family Circle Magazine*. It was a heart-warming scene that embraced everyone in the church. "Onward Christian soldiers marching as to war . . ."

The modest building was decorated with simple trappings. Silk robes and religious accoutrements adorned the walls. David noticed the ornate chains, enema bags, and horsehair shirts and his suspicions were aroused. Black drapes at the front of the hall slid open to reveal a large stage and a reverent pall descended on the audience like storm clouds. A huge, neon sign blinked to life and illuminated the church with red-and-white crackling light. The sign read, "The Holy Temple of Connubial Bliss." An announcement snapped and chortled over the PA system, "The Reverend Michael Kinship is here with Brothers Pierce and Sharp Shears. Welcome Brethren to the Golden Crucifixion Review with The Avenging Angels and the All-nudie cast of Sinners and Saints!"

Beneath the neon sign stood The Erect Cross in the shape of a large, golden cock. A block of black marble lay in front of the cross like an altar. Reverend Kinship stood at a pulpit near the front of the stage. He was immaculately dressed in black, enclosed within an ermine cape like a bug in a cocoon. He carried a whip in one hand and a bible in the other. The Brothers Pierce and Sharp Shears solemnly stood behind the Reverend. They were wearing dog collars, the latest fashion craze, to enhance their leather apparel. David looked around and noticed each person in the audience had a golden cock on a chain that they fondled, licked, and snorted in a gesture that seemed to fortify their religious experience.

A gang of neon-clad musicians sashayed across the stage and stood by the altar. They started the show with a boomerang tribute to Marilyn Manson. Splashing color transformed the church into a gyrating kaleidoscope. A gaggle of naked cheerleaders hobbled around the stage, clapping hands and yelling, "Hallelujah!" The overture concluded with a tender rock version of "Nearer My Lord to Thee."

An Insurmountable Sermon

The holy Michael Kinship cleared his throat and began the sermon, "Welcome sisters and brethren. I want to talk with you this evening about our relationship to the Lord Jesus Christ. He died for our sins! Jesus died for our sins! Do you . ." The reverend paused for effect, and then continued, "Do you know what that means? I'll tell you what it means -- it means that Jesus didn't want to live! That's right, brethren, Jesus Christ died because he did not want to live for our sins!

"My God, my holy God -- I can feel Jesus in me this very moment. I can feel Jesus dying inside of me for my sins! I feel it! I feel the pain of death! How many out there can **Feel** Christ's pain? It isn't easy to *feeel* the Lord's pain . . . but, brothers and sisters, that's what the Lord wants for all of us -- to *feeel* his pain! He wants us all to get down on our knees in blissful agony."

The people in the audience began to sob and sniff their golden cocks. Tears glistened in the minister's eyes as he continued, "Everybody please, get down on your knees. I want to tell you something about Jesus. The Lord Jesus chose to be crucified. He was brutally nailed to the cross, stoned, whipped, and jabbed with spears. Jesus chose pain and torture for **us** -- to show the way to Salvation.

In Matthew, Chapter 5, Jesus says, 'Blessed are ye when men shall revile you and persecute you and say all manner of evil against you falsely, for my sake.' That means, my children, that Jesus wants us to seek pain in order to revile our sins. In fact, our sin is our pain. Jesus doesn't tell us to stop sinning -- he tells us to love pain! Sin adds to our pain. So I say unto you my children, that it is all right to be corrupt and corruptible. Yea, it is blessed as long as we suffer! It is blessed to choose pain as did our Lord Jesus Christ. Christ in his mercy gave us the godly gift of suffering.

"In Matthew, Chapter 10, Jesus says, Think not that I am come to send peace on earth. I came not to send peace, but a sword.' He came with a sword to bring pain and suffering. We must follow the Lord's example and bring suffering to one another. We must, in solemn reverence and with love for Jesus, incur the gift of exquisite pain to our fellow man." Tears flowed down the reverend's cheeks while the naked cheerleaders whimpered and sobbed. The Brothers Pierce and Sharp Shears fell to their knees and obsequiously licked the minister's boots.

"Brothers and sisters I know you are looking forward to the main event of the evening and so am I. Soon we will be visited by the Avenging Angels and with the help of God we will be privileged to participate in tonight's Crucifixion. Before we begin, let me take this opportunity to announce the '*getting to know you*' dance for all the youngsters in our congregation which will take place in the basement after tonight's main event. As usual we will be serving coffee and cake in the vestry. Blessings upon you. Let us pray."

Sounds of motorcycles filled the auditorium. The audience cheered and sang, "Onward Christian Soldiers." Two monster cycles roared onto the stage. Several Hell's Angels dismounted from their metal beasts. They were dragging a gagged victim. They proceeded to strip and chain him to the altar. He was helpless and extremely beautiful, a very slim young man with shaggy hair and the perfect features of a Greek athlete, an alabaster statue come to life. Sudden recognition clamped down on David's mind with fear and horror. He knew the boy. He was a Numan, a true angel.

Clean, scrubbed teenagers passed collection baskets. David stood to leave. He couldn't watch any longer. There was nothing he could do to stop the insanity. A young usher accosted him, "Don't you want to see the crucifixion?" The alien vomited in the collection basket and left.

Clandestine Meetings in Strange Places

The L.A. art museum looked like a giant complex of monumental blocks sinking into the La Brea Tar Pits, a perfect reconstruction. Three main buildings sloped at odd angles toward one another. Everything inside the buildings was lopsided because the floors sank and no surface was level. The buildings were no longer maintained because quicksand was discovered under the structural foundation. Most art critics agreed that sinking buildings were far more aesthetic than the original construction. David couldn't find Aramet Yashafats, so he took a tour of the latest artistic revelations.

The show was entitled, "Primal Art: The First and Last Form." The first piece he approached was called "Primal Statement" by artist, Jack Litch. A compact mound of feces was displayed within a pristine cube of Plexiglas -- blunt and simple. In a video presentation, Litch talked about his work, "I can't control my primal statements. I have to let go no matter where I am -- and that's when my art is the most spontaneous and brilliant. I never coax my art like some 'pretend artists' who use laxatives and other performance enhancement drugs. My art is completely natural and unrestrained."

Everything in the collection was an extension of the "Primal Statement." Some of the paintings were total sensory experiences, sculpted surfaces with muted colors and pungent odors. One painting even talked, emitting a loud, low-pitched sound like escaping air. Critics praised the show.

David began to worry -- where was his contact. He walked through the exhibit a second time and noticed a scrap of paper under a hill of manure. The paper was not part of the sculpture so he discretely snatched it and stealthily glanced at the note, "Sorry I couldn't wait. The art stank too much. I'll meet you at the Prison Camp south of Market where we can exchange information." The note was signed, "Fats." David was anxious to leave the museum.

Walking Backward

He walked several miles to get to the rendezvous. He was becoming more paranoid by the minute. Eyes were drilling holes in the back of his head. David followed an indirect route through back alleys and underground parking-garages. He conjured memories to take his mind off the imminent sense of danger. He recalled a long lost friend named

Adam. At one time they had been intimate, exchanging vital information and protecting one another. Adam was a mutant. His brain was fried in a failed lab experiment at Harvard. He had a Ph.D. in quantum physics. Since the accident he couldn't relate to people, only to his dog "Scrounge." For years he lived with his dog in a broken-down Ford.

Everyone made Adam paranoid. He was afraid to work and afraid to apply for any kind of assistance. He stole canned food from stores and cooked on the radiator of his car. He understood mechanics and made repairs to keep moving and escaping from enemy agents. He moved from gas station to public restroom where he and Scrounge could drink water from the sink. He never shaved or bathed. Everyday he became more like his dog in appearance and attitude. He truly loved Scrounge. Dog and man were inseparable. David never knew where his friend got money for gas -- he was afraid to panhandle. Somehow he kept going, driving his old Ford -- until the oil prices changed everything. First there was an embargo, years later it was speculators, and finally oil companies gained control of the government. There was no way Adam could keep up with the price of gas so he had to park. Man and dog were sitting ducks. They became casualties of the *Cheney Machine*, ground up like fodder and thrown to sharks while oil magnates drilled the whole ocean floor for black crude.

Alien Links in a Chain

The Prison Camp was a bar, a "fantasy prison" for men. Brick walls and steel cages created a distinctive atmosphere. Country-and-Western "Muzak" droned from plastic speakers. The intoxicating smell of leather and booze wafted through the smoke-clogged air. The place was a pleasure factory reflecting the most popular trend in postal-modern interior design. The alien was able to detect what was hidden behind the chic camouflage: this was an undercover drop-spot and link to the Underbelly.

He witnessed the "fun buns" contest where secret information was communicated to clandestine agents working for various power brokers. Ten men stood on a plank displaying rippling muscles. In unison the men turned with a jaunty kick. The MC flashed his gold caps and snapped a playful whip. The ten men dropped their leather draws, wriggling like snakes shedding skin. Assholes were revealed. David's third eye beamed, searching for privy information. The MC commented and sampled the assets. The audience cheered, drank, and began to fumble and fiddle. Each ass on stage was judged. The best ass was selected and personally inspected by everyone in the bar. Information was shared. The ass was probed and tested, assaulted and molested.

The ass situation led to an intimate free-for-all -- deep probing as agents were squashed together and fumbled for information. David was not the only spy. Everyone was suspicious, groping for identities, feeling for assets. Where was Aramet Yashafats?

A young man was slowly being molested. His face glowed with seraphic innocence and insatiable lust. One "prison-guard" was shoving his jackhammer down the boy's throat while a faux prisoner pushed a thunder-club up his ass. The youth glowed within a sheen of silver sweat. David recognized him. He was the same one, the Numan sacrificed on the altar in the church.

Lights flickered warning everyone to stop. The patrons turned to stone beneath the purple haze of black lights. Music began again, droning wails from a horror film that reanimated the statues. Everyone started prancing and bowing, jumping through space, delicately hoping around the floor -- magnificent pirouettes and expertly executed leaps. Old men and young were dancing together, dildos held high. A faux-slave got waxed on a rack. A prisoner was fist-fucked in plain sight. A row of men was drenched in urine. The love dance was intense -- causing an information-overload. The alien was floundering in an ancient cave of Sybarites searching for the Oracle that would reveal the location of his lost Psyche.

The air shimmered with static electricity and the earth shifted beneath David's feet as Arabian Music seduced his senses. Romantic images wafted through his mind on scented clouds of Shalimar. Peeking through a thousand colored-veils he saw a fat sultan surrounded by one hundred concubines. David was envious. Suddenly zealots invaded the palace. They stared at the alien, lusting for his blood. They were terrorists. The groups were all the same: Arabs, Jews, Blacks, Gays, Whites -- programmed for violence. There was a fatwa with David's name on it. He didn't know why they wanted him, perhaps because he was an alien or just because he was in the wrong place. Slowly they surrounded David, pushing him up against the wall of veils. "We don't need weapons," they leered, "we can rid the Earth of you with our bare hands!"

"Please, man," David screamed, "I don't want your crummy desert." It was the wrong thing to say.

They moved closer, mouths open as if they wanted to eat the alien alive. His plunger was his only weapon, but David could only use it one time (the battery needed recharging). Anyway he had other plans for his plunger. He had a bigger target then a band of sex-crazed lunatics and raving fanatics. In the midst of the attack, David realized he planned to confront the *Controller* and he would need his weapon.

"Howdy, man -- you look like you is in trouble," beamed a sallow face.

"Fats -- glad to see you!"

The assailants looked stunned by the intrusion, but they weren't about to back down.

"I'll hold them off with my switchblade while you escape between my legs. Best you stay undercover for the rest of the night. These bastards are out to get your ass. Go to the Calabash Hotel, south of the Slot. Tell Leona The Domina that Aramet Fats sent you." He kept flashing his knife in the faces of the enemy to keep them at bay while he talked, "don't stay in a room -- too dangerous. Keep awake all night and walk the halls. Meet me at dawn in restroom 609 on the Exxon-Mobile Beach. Hurry, man, get down between my legs -- they're about to attack."

As David knelt between Yashafats' legs he heard him yell from a great distance, "Go down, man -- and, good lu-u-c-k-k!"

Mistaken Identity

The alien fell into a matrix of colors and sounds. Traffic screamed and he was almost run down by an electric paddle-bus. Hordes of people and genetic-prototypes walked or hobbled over the paving stones on Market Street. A huge man with a puffing, stovepipe mouth drove a herd of chained children through the crowd. Tags around their necks identified them as unwanted babies, orphans from Rwanda, Iraqi survivors, aborted embryos and eunuchs -- all to be sold at auction.

David felt nauseous, but his body needed some nourishment before finding the Calabash -- no telling when he'd have another chance to eat. The restaurants were crowded. Each cheap diner was trying to grab customers with garish colors that oozed off the walls and into the street. Screaming teenagers were scarfing down burgers and humping beneath red, Formica tables.

He walked into the first twenty-four hour nightmare that called to him, "Hey man, how bout something to eat. Cum on in!" The place was spotless. Busboys hustled ass, scrubbing away at every plastic surface. David walked to the order counter and surveyed the talking menu. The 3-D pictures of food made him squeamish. Everything was covered with flowing whipped-cream and fried to perfection. A girl dressed in a party hat and scanty red-halter addressed David, "Hi, I'm Ruthie. Can I help you?" Her hands were inside her halter fumbling with her breasts. She smiled graciously, "please, can I help you!"

He ordered a big dog, which was delivered instantly. Everything tasted like processed Styrofoam. Munching-songs screamed over the speakers, "Squeeze my crotch and love me hard. Rock my basket like a tub of lard." Big dog finished, David ordered a cup of coffee from a skinny waiter with acne and green eyes that stared with disturbing intensity. "Mister would you like to toast some buttered buns?" David wasn't certain what he meant. Perhaps he had information to exchange. The alien wondered if he had found another Underbelly connection so he accepted the offer.

He joined the waiter in the blue-tiled, graffiti-yellowed men's room. A grizzled wino was lying in a pool of urine on the floor. They had to slide the wino against the wall to make room to maneuver. The boy rolled his tongue, his lean body exploding inside his skin-tight uniform. David could feel heat pouring off the waiter's body like a volcano. The boy leaned over the sink and fiddled with his belt. He dropped his pants and hiked up his shirt. His beautiful, hard buns were exposed. The crack of his ass was slick and greasy. He humped the sink and spread his cheeks.

"Quick, mister, stick it in before my boss starts yelling at me." He was sweating profusely, "mister, I got to have it. Do you want a blowjob? I'm so damn horny I'll do anything." He whined and pleaded. "Mister, I've been shoving everything I can get up my ass -- hotdogs, burgers -- but it doesn't work. I need a cock. I'll pay. Please, man."

David was repelled by the situation and the young man's insistent pleas. The information was damaged, as if a virus infected the code. He stared at the waiter's beautiful ass. Spots popped before his eyes. Blood-and-puss sores erupted on his smooth, taut flesh -- scabs formed and hardened. Sex parasites, worm heads with teeth, emerged from his asshole. The boy was a venel addict, a schmecker -- probably totally unaware that he had contacted the disease. He didn't know his ass was turning into an infected hole. The boy tried to grab David as he left. David heard the addict's nasal whine as he offered himself to the wino -- he fearfully reflected on the burgers and dogs the waiter had pushed up his ass.

Hiding in Limbo

The Calabash Hotel was a green door in a purple fog near the wharf. Slow moving creatures appeared to slink through the thick haze. Grotesque silhouettes loomed large against ancient brick walls. Something was happening behind the door. His alien senses picked up strains of music; old-fashioned dance-hall melodies: an eerie, muted whine from the Depression Era and the hopeless optimism of a lady Blues Singer.

He knocked. A cleft in the door chinked open.

"Yes."

David replied, "Fats sent me, Aramet Yashafats."

"Yes."

"I need a place to hide. I don't want a room."

"Yes. Thirty bills. No questions asked."

He slipped the money through the cleft. The door swung open. The place was dark and musty. The *thing* before him was an apparition that stunk from formaldehyde.

"I am Leona The Domina. I am neither man or woman nor human thing. I am death given life. If you wish you may use my body. If not, seek refuge in the caverns of Calabash for I may seek revenge."

David stared at the apparition, which appeared to shift before his eyes. It quivered between a parody of Marlene Dietrich and Boris Karloff. It wore black-mesh stockings and a lace corset. It held a wax mask. The wax impression was stark: white as bone with a slashed mouth and purple eyes. David received the distinct impression that the face behind the mask was damaged, the result of an accident with an acetylene torch.

"Yes . . . my face is ugly. I wear this mask to hide what I consider beautiful."

"Is it really your desire to make love to me?" He hesitantly questioned.

"No! I want you to use me. We can use one another."

The thought of her proposition made him queasy, "No! I paid the entrance fee -- that's as far as I'll go."

"Then, heed my warning. There will come a time when you will be forced to discard your own mask -- and confront your real face. Now -- get lost!"

He wandered from floor to floor and through the halls and tunnels of Calabash. Each hall was exactly the same. There were ten doors along the left side of each passage. The wall without doors was covered with faded red-velvet. Ancient gas lamps illuminated the hallways. David still heard music coming from far away, ancient ballads, serenades, and a never-ending waltz. Unfamiliar creatures flitted back and forth across his path. He imagined cat-like animals with long needle-snouts and tiny bat wings. He saw several dogs walking like men. David questioned his sanity because the dogs appeared to be drinking wine from crystal goblets while they caressed a naked girl who crawled on all fours. Fear intensified at the sight of an enormous "Smegma Fish" walking on four spindly legs, staring with bulging eyes and menacing teeth. It made lewd sounds as it moved towards David like a phantom from some alien hell. Sucking vapors escaped from doors that mysteriously opened and closed. There were no windows. The walls were closing in. There was no end to the passageways. They led nowhere in an endless labyrinth.

He didn't know how long he wandered -- hours, perhaps days. He heard disturbing voices: incomplete conversations, snickering, unsettling laughter. He fell into a trance, sleep walking in an alien dream. Other people were also walking in a trance. A blond man in a leather jumpsuit with a red scarf around his neck wore one skate and shuffled down the hall. David saw a magnificent beast with golden feathers and the head of a lion.

An apathetic girl was brutally assaulted by two men who looked like enormous apes. She never blinked and made no sounds. The alien saw an angel lurking in a dark doorway. When he approached, the creature disappeared into the room. David peered through the keyhole to witness a landscape of distorted formations leading to an ancient cave. The angel was waiting for him in that cavern.

David peered into several keyholes; each one was a magic lens revealing incredible, often terrifying, scenes. In one room he saw five-year-old children having an orgy, exhibiting the lusts and passions of adults. Another keyhole showed two blobs of liquid-flesh having sex. They talked like ordinary people. One was called Dick and the other was Jane. In another room, he saw Max and his teenage daughter. Max puffed on a cigar. His belly overshadowed his tiny penis. Jenny, his daughter, had small breasts that looked like scoops of vanilla ice cream. Max spanked Jenny and taught her how to be a good, little whore. David peeked through another lens and saw a vision floating in mid-air like God with a halo, beard, and sorrowful eyes. David witnessed the man's lacerated flesh. He was chained to a rack and called out, "beat me, please!"

He hurried through the halls, fascinated by strange enigmas. Synthesized males with bulbous cocks pranced like proud colts. Women with penises fucked men with vaginas. Severed sex organs crawled across mildewed floors. Desire was everywhere. The rooms behind the doors called to David Oblivion.

He peered through a keyhole in a brown, stained door and saw a cage for a madman: brick walls with no windows and a gray concrete floor. In one corner, several black candles burned and dripped into a mound of formless wax. Skulls wavered in the tenuous candlelight and leered at David. Oddly shaped boxes and ornate chests of various sizes were scattered on the floor. A stained mattress lay opposite the dripping candles. An androgynous boy sat on the mattress and fondled a large wooden box. He had smooth, copper skin, dark eyes and black hair. His lips were like strips of red fruit.

The boy was naked. His compact body shimmered in the dim light. His eyes glowed like mirrors reflecting miraculous dreams. He was very young -- no body hair, only a black patch surrounding his extended penis. David watched as he placed the box on the mattress and crawled over it with his whole body, tenderly stroking the wood. He arched like a cat and touched his belly to the box. His penis was very hard as it slid along the wooden edge. David heard the boy murmur as if he were delirious, "My thing -- My beautiful thing." His voice sounded like soft singing.

As if in a trance, the boy opened the box. David's mind recoiled from what he saw, but he was paralyzed -- forced to watch a large "Bulla Maggot" emerge from the box. The boy's eyes glowed like black coals, hypnotized. The maggot's gelatinous head was a mass of fish scales, dripping eyes and sucker holes. The Bulla appeared to get larger as it rose out of the box. Maggot hissed. Boy stroked the festering head . . . kissed, licked and sucked the maggot's vitreous brain.

His young cock was hard and pulsing. The Bulla emitted needle-tendrils and drove them into his tender body. The boy choked a scream. Red spots appeared where tendrils pierced his flesh. The Bulla lifted itself above the pain stricken boy. Masses of liquid flesh, entrails and slime overflowed from the box. The distraught alien could smell the ancient rot of an oceanic graveyard. The boy reached out to caress the creature. The giant fish-maggot wrapped itself around the boy. David heard the slurping sounds of ghastly love.

The young body pulsated in the throes of a seizure within the coils of the maggot. The paralyzed alien watched the Bulla force itself into the boy's ass. David would never forget the sound of the boy's scream. The Bulla plunged into the anus -- filmy, odorous coil-after-coil slipped into his ass. David watched in transfixed horror as the maggot's dripping body was swallowed by the anal cavity. The youth was delirious, his stomach bloated and swollen. Blood began to shoot from his mouth. His cock throttled, belched, and spurted a continuous flow of gushing semen. Black worms swam in the jism.

The horrible sound, the screaming, ended when the Bulla ripped through the boy's throat. It tore through bones and flesh, and wore the boy's body like a gruesome garment. The Bulla shot across the room like a giant serpent and David found himself staring into a yellow, watery fish-eye. He jumped away from the door and ran down the hall. The maggot escaped from the cell. David looked back and saw the Bulla attack the apathetic girl. She was screaming, brought back to her senses by the overwhelming horror.

David ran. Everything was distorted. The walls became soft, pliable. The floor rolled like the slimy back of a serpent. Lights flickered and dimmed. He stumbled into the lower caverns. He heard footsteps running behind him, chasing him. Hands reached out to grab him. He saw the giant Bulla slithering toward him. Leona's wax mask flew through the air, shrieking. David saw himself in a thousand shattered mirrors limping like a monster in the night. A luminous Numan with silver wings stood just beyond his reach. The labyrinth sheltered the Minotaur, twice as big as any man with a three-foot hard-on. The bull-man was coming to split the alien in half. David was too exhausted to move. He was trapped -- escape was not possible, but with that realization the walls dissolved leaving David wondering if the Calabash ever existed. The fog lifted. He could see the sun. Dawn had arrived.

Alien Caught on Camera at Beach Resort

The beach was crowded at dawn. No one slept in the city. The morning-light pierced the jagged, metal arms of the amusement park that rose above the sand. The "Viagra Fun-Center" spread for miles along the beach, eating the coast like an insatiable amoeba. Flashing logos were everywhere, invitations to new and exciting thrill rides. There were twenty monster roller coasters in various stages of disrepair. Whirling dervish psycho-pods thrust squealing patrons into oblivion. Some fun seekers never returned from their piston-blast to ecstasy -- left hanging in a tipsy gondola or digested by meshing gears. There was a constant rhythm and shifting of explosive energy. The laughing-lady mannequin never stopped shrieking. Sideshow freaks led crowds through a pinball maze of deadly hi-jinx.

The area of the Fun Center, which had collapsed, was like a graveyard at the bottom of the sea. David spied watery lights shifting like underwater currents. Twisted scraps of metal were heaped in mounds like the skeletal remains of sunken ships. Mutants, addicts and schmeckers hid in the debris, stealing and killing to survive.

The Exxon-Mobile Beach was black from generations of oil sludge, tar and garbage trampled into the sand by billions of eager feet. The air was an oppressive blanket that overwhelmed David's sinuses. Crowds of people lived in the mire. Grand hotels for wealthy tourists appeared to languish and sink along the horizon where the beach met concrete. The beach was a resort where people came to experience new sensations and erotic stimulation. Young and old hustled and screwed beneath the crumbling piers. Stone towers stood like erect cocks all along the shore, fully equipped with missiles, guns, and militia. They protected the Free Sex Sector from invading navies. Restrooms were haphazardly scattered along the beach where encounters were arranged between tourists, spies, and military personnel. Enormous lobsters guarded the shoreline. They were bright turquoise harmless-hybrids large as buildings, glowing like beacons in the night.

David pushed his way through crowds of spectators. Everyone was watching the "Miss Millennium Parade," a mock rendition of the 1959 "Miss America Pageant." Girls with painted faces and bouffant hairdos floated down the boardwalk in white Thunderbirds. Cinematic overlays on each face created the appropriate "smiling" illusion and voices were reproduced from authentic recordings. The girls wore one-piece bathing costumes and clutched plastic roses. Male replicas in tuxedos accompanied them. Baton twirlers, marching bands, and vendors created a realistic drama that energized everyone. The alien searched for restroom 609 where he was supposed to meet Yashafats. Lovely bodies pushed back. Everyone was horny. Flesh sizzled in the cool dawn.

He paid the entrance toll and stumbled into 609 feeling ravaged. His clothes were disheveled and spotted with stains. The bathroom was packed with male-female bodies in various stages of undress. David heard the slurping sounds of information being exchanged. He felt wet, sloppy tongues caress his body as he pushed through the mob of sailors, executives, housewives, and teens. He felt ambushed. They wanted to suck-out his alien identity and drain him of his essence. In defense, David mounted a counter attack, foraging for codes and useful statistics. In the midst of his slurping, he noticed a series of taps, a foot message directed at the alien. He recognized Fats and tapped an answering jig. A piece of paper fluttered in his direction. It read like a fortune cookie, "Ah, the sweet mystery of life. What you seek is at the Celestial Orifice -- go there! It's been nice knowing you, farewell. Arafesh Mesh." He was puzzled by the altered name, but he didn't linger.

The Celestial Orifice was the hub between the beach and the amusement park -- a palatial bar, casino, and tearoom constructed in the grand style of Twenty-first Century "Art-Decline" overlooking the ocean. David thought it looked like an enormous, stained-glass pustule. The celestial shambles heaved itself into the sky like a spiral layer cake. Neon cubes rose in disarray, connected to an Assyrian pavilion with gold minarets -- crowned by a ponderous crystal turret. Dancing waters spit from fountains in the overflowing moat that surrounded the massive construction. Tahitian torches burned around the outside of the moat. The complex was illuminated with garish strobe-signs: "Hot!" "Sexy!" "Repulsive!" "Exciting!" "Bizarro!"

A hologram sky-relief called "Screwing in Space" encircled the Celestial Orifice like a firmament of hot flesh. Giant sex-dolls made from plastic adorned the mud-soaked pathways leading to the Orifice. The statues were animated to simulate sexual positions inspired by the Karma sutra.

David paid the entrance fee, pushed through the appropriate passageway, and shuffled into the Orifice. In the process, he slipped into an alien time-warp, somewhere between moments where everything appeared frozen. The time-warp only lasted an instant so he had to work quickly. David was familiar with the Orifice and felt relatively safe amidst the opulent decrepitude. It was like returning to a welcoming womb on the shore of a polluted, fog-bank sea.

The main gallery was called the "Hole of Glory" and it was an immense, shapeless room. A long, curved bar ambled through the room like a snake, flexing its way in and around groups of people. Old style projection-screens hung from the ceiling playing faded videos of dead celebrities. Large digital-mirrors were placed throughout the room flashing images of customers in embarrassing situations. A verdant, plastic-forest clung to the walls under layers of dust and cobwebs. The dance floor was a huge black-circle and the ceiling was sprayed with flecks of silver glitter.

Beneath the plastic ferns, the walls were covered with graffiti and pictures torn from antiquated porno-magazines. A glass partition separated the dance floor from a long line of toilets. A naked boy sat on each toilet with his left leg chained to a taximeter. A red neon-sign hung over the toilets, "Pay as you go BLOW! With lipstick $20 more. Use correct change. These mouths are specially trained to give the best service in town! Please, no screwing at this concession. Pump-holes and fuck-racks are located in Bung Hall. Kooch Girls are waiting upstairs in the Golden Labia Ballroom. Remember, every night is orgy night in the Platinum Vulva Lounge. Price of admission includes a free smorgasbord. Enjoy, enjoy!"

The toilet boys were very attractive. Men and women waited in long lines in front of each toilet to get sucked off while they stuffed money in the meters.

The place was still frozen in the alien time warp. Liquor was suspended in air. Dancers were caught in mid step. Each person was posed like an exotic statue. A woman wore a silver dress cut open to reveal her vagina. A tall man with a shaved head wore a transparent gown. A drag queen was dressed like a garden of daisies with living hummingbirds attached to the petals by tiny silver wires.

Time began to return. Everyone started moving in slow motion. A frog man did a slow-motion summersault with a loud, bellowing croak. Blaring music groaned, "sexx maasheen . . . gett onn uppp." People moved slowly to the moaning music, dancing a pavane. Gold-lame frock coats and purple raiment drifted and floated like elaborate birds. Eyes glowed unnaturally and scarlet lips opened expectantly.

For an instant everything moved faster than normal. Teenage meth-freaks hit each other like punching bags. Dancers moved like cartoon characters. The music sounded like an insect band in a tin can. The light was like white puffballs exploding on David's alien eyes. People lined up for blowjobs like clicking tin soldiers. At the bar wind-up dolls ordered booze, "blah, blah," threw money on bar, left tip, drank booze, and started over. A fat fairy flew through the room like a popped balloon. An angry woman screamed. Then, it ended and normal time returned.

It was 7 a.m. and everyone was dressed in immaculate drag. Flesh-tone make-up was perfect, all eyes were aglow and every hair was in place. People stayed in the Orifice all night, but they were preserved with plastic seal to look their best. The alien was greeted by a reconstituted Lady Divine wearing a blood-red dress that complemented her copious figure.

"I am divine!" She stated.

"I know . . . I've adored you from afar," David diplomatically replied.

"How sweet. Would you like some bonbons? They're poisoned, of course."

"I appreciate the offer, but I'll stick with a drink."

"Pity, pity. Oh well, you're cute -- rather like an alien monster."

David was about to speak when someone intruded, "Hey, I'll have a bonbon, lady. I never got sumpin' for nothin' before."

Divine gave the man a candy and he immediately doubled over and gagged. He dropped to the floor, thrashing like an epileptic. Divine chortled, "Isn't it marvelous -- but it won't kill him, poor thing -- just enough strychnine to make him deathly ill for several days. He'll love it!"

The alien left Divine to her playful tricks and sat at a table near the window. He watched the dancers. Someone in a penis costume bobbed up-and-down simulating masturbation. A DJ burst a blood vessel over the loud speakers, "Hey, hey, hey. This is station U-M-P-A -- umpa, umpa, umpa. I know you know what that means. Hey, hey. This is your very own cute DJ, Robin Red-Bird with my jaybird haircut and my every-ready bird-dog -- Woof, woof. I'm hot with lots to play -- and lots to play with -- all day! Here's a record flash called *Dancing Machine* by those five de-li-cious Choc-o-lites -- um, um."

Dancers shouted and leaped. David watched a group of naked waiters with identical bodies and tousled hair selling drinks and favors on the dance floor.

"Hey, hey. This is your friendly jock with a hot-flash for you. There's going to be a 'Fuckin-A' dancing marathon right here, today. Right-O -- now's your chance to dance and fuck. Winner gets all. Hey, hey -- right now in the Forni-torium don't miss the sex-slave auction. This is a Millennium Special. Save today only -- ten percent off on all slaves. And, now, here's a record express hit, *Do It Till You're*

Satisfied."

David recognized Max and daughter from the Calabash. Max was playing cards with two friends. They were all paunchy and well fed. Max pushed Jenny under the table and told her to get busy. A buxom cowboy grabbed a pretty waiter on the dance floor. The young man protested. The cowboy unhitched his big dick and thrust it at the boy. Another playful cowboy joined the fun. The loudspeaker warned the cowboys, "You gotta pay for that kind of action. Please stop!" The cowboys and waiter gingerly rolled on the floor without heeding the warning. Grunge, the mutant bouncer, lumbered into the room. The floor shook. Grunge was a five hundred pound Ox-man with eight arms. He grabbed the cowboys and lifted them at arms length, ten feet apart. Cowboys were dazed. Grunge smashed them together until they become one inseparable mass of flesh and blood.

"Hey, hey, hey," the disc jockey crooned, "a little too much fun in the arena. Remember we all gotta pay if we wanna play. Ha, ha.

"I wanna tell you about a surprise. At noon, today, the Celestial Orifice presents the Flesh Peckers Sex-Band. They're hot, really hot. Not only do they play instruments, but these cute peckers play each other. Did you ever see an electric-solo suck a nine inch organ? Wow! How about a singing asshole? Too much! It's really an orgy of sound. Noon, today!

"Right now, I've got a thousand year-old favorite . . . old Boris in the lab doin' *The Monster Mash*."

Everyone did the "Deca-Dance." Crowds of people mingled, rotated and shifted through the giant Orifice.

The singing streets were empty. Everyone had returned home to perform Last Rites. The city of rose-quartz and purple amethyst was dying. Olden-Fohr, the scholar, was responsible for the demise. He sought the Oracle -- the Crystal Skull. It wasn't difficult to attain the talisman; he merely made a pact with demons.

The Skull appeared to breathe as it glowed brighter then dimmer. Olden was forsaken by everyone in the city. While they mourned, he waited. No one sought vengeance or revenge. They knew he was already a prisoner. Even Omnoc, Olden's beloved companion, left him by means of suicide -- but it was Olden's misguided actions that really killed him.

He was alone with the unholy Skull of Time. Images dilated in the crystal eyes. The jaw opened and closed with contrite finality. The future revolved in the translucent brain. Olden-Fohr witnessed more misery than any mortal could bear, but he was unable to tear his eyes away. The world became a holocaust of endless war. The malign Skull leered accusingly. It made clucking sounds that ripped into his brain. Olden was the man who unveiled the future and set it in motion. He could not die, but forever remained outside of time to witness the devastation.

"Do you wanna drink, a fuck, or an enema. You can't sit at this table with an empty glass. You gotta be a paying customer," shouted a naked eunuch with red hair holding a silver tray.

"Bring me a drink -- something strong and cheap."

He was brought the most expensive drink on the menu. David felt ripped off and refused to tip. The eunuch bent over and farted. David slapped his ass causing him to shriek and run away.

The place was a mass of crowded activity and conversation. David turned up his alien sensitivities. It was like fishing in a hot, sticky hole looking for information, hairs got in the way and the smell was rank. He'd been directed here to get answers. He listened for clues.

"If you want it silky, wet and tight, you'll find it in our Wet Dream Shop."

"Charley -- he ate the friggin tits right off her and she didn't bat an eye."

"The Enema Bar is open for your pleasure and convenience."

"Three. I tell you she had three new tits dangling like sacks of mashed potatoes."

"Jack! I've got The Grunge. I'm being eaten alive. I'm on fire. Oh, oh, I've never felt anything like this. It's too good!"

"Don't miss the special buyer's sale in the Rectum Lounge -- wholesale prices on twenty-four inch dildos complete with feelers, spikes, razors, and thorns."

"Why, yes -- I have a whole *synchro-mime* family. I guess I collect relatives the same way people used to collect antiques."

"They say they've spotted strange lights over New Fuckland. It must be them new flying assholes."

His mind was becoming entangled in idle conversations. The outside world was beginning to infiltrate. His alien brain was fragmenting and he couldn't hold the world together for much longer.

"I wonder where the yellow went."

"I tell you -- it started in a place called, Old Jerusalem. The war fanned out like a bonfire."

"I like my lips to look delicious, not dry."

"I was born with icky hair."

The talk was corrosive and he couldn't concentrate -- too many negative distractions. David was stunned like a deer caught in the headlights of an oncoming truck. All he could do was watch.

The Celestial Orifice spun and fell like a bizarre carousel, a moving panorama of characters and events. Through it all, David's search continued for the missing link, the vital information necessary to fit all the pieces of the puzzle together.

Twenty Nubian slaves carried golden Cleopatra on an arc of sapphire flowers. Giant toad-men sang praises to her glory. A reanimated Cecil B. DeMille directed the jarring spectacle. Everyone was a composite of cinematic illusions composed of projected images. Voices were dubbed. Soundtracks jumbled and spliced. The production was out-of-synch, but the performance never stopped.

At the next table David watched a man stuff himself with food. He had an incredible horse-face. He ate fried sweetmeats gorged with grease. A sex slave sat under his chair. The slave was a pot licker. Horse-face sat without pants, his naked ass bobbed through a hole in the seat of the chair.

David recognized Ezra Cobb from the movie, "Deranged." He was sitting with the corpse of his mother. He enjoyed the nutritional value of his victims. He was a pop-culture favorite elevated to the status of hero by the Zeitgeist Brain.

Reverend Kinship was giving a sermon about the evils of mercy while he carved holy pictures into the flesh of a naked acolyte. Dancing girls flayed each other with whips. Leona the Domina did the Charleston with the Minotaur. The Bulla Maggot slinked along the top of the bar wearing the bloody carcass of a victim. Enemy agents drifted in-and-out like vapors. David spied Mrs. Homily waving a crucifix and holding a dead chicken. A severed stump with one eye painfully hobbled across the dance floor. The "Miss America" beauty queens glided through the room in a long, smiling procession. Rigid zombies, newly revived, drank cocktails and gossiped about the past.

A large stage was lowered from the ceiling like a beached whale. The Flesh Peckers leaped onto the back of the whale in an electric flash of thunderous sound. They striped off their purple g-strings and gyrated to ejaculation riffs. Four pretty boys played guitar, sax, and cum-drums; two comely girls played synthesizers and a selection of dildos. The group yelled to the crowd, "are you ready for the 'Fuckin-A Dancin-Contest'? Alright! Let's hoedown -- whip out your dick and unlatch your clit. Hee Haw!"

The dance floor was a typhoon of thumping and humping. The girls on stage worked up a froth of excitement with their dildos, while the boys did a Johnny-ass, Fucking-axe routine. The act was very hot and spicy. They sang, "Rock-n-fuck. Just stick it in until you bust. Rock-n-fuck and rock-n-roll . . ." The crowd went mad, pumping and chugging. David recognized famous artist, Jack Litch. He was so excited he created a spontaneous shit. Everyone was overwhelmed. Bodies glistened with jism and sweat.

A huge rat leaped across the dance floor followed by a maniac with a bloody hand. In the same instant David saw a face that seemed to glow. He looked like the boy in the church. They recognized one another. At last, the alien would meet the Numan. He ached to touch his soft hair, curling like waves of umber clouds. They would exchange information, grow together and find enlightenment. But David clung to his doubts -- could he/she really accept an *alien*. He was jolted out of his reverie by flashing battle-lights and blasting war-sirens.

People were running, crashing into walls and hiding under tables. The war syndrome was everywhere. Onslaught was always introduced by howls and shrieks. The invasion began: Captain Dork and his sex-starved pirates crashed through the roof. Ruby the Dyke and the Hoary Fairy tightened up the rear flanks. The Fairy madly fucked a dwarf's hump. The Orifice gasped and groaned. "Whump! Thud! Thwack! Crunch!" The Flesh Peckers jerked-off and sang, "Kung Fu fighting it's really frightening, but so exciting. Kung Fu fighting. Whoa, Whaa!"

Ruby the Dyke yelled, "I need a new bag of smelly peckers for me and the girls."

Hoary Fairy chimed in, "Um, me too, me too!"

Captain Dork spun on his peg leg and yelled, "Har, I want me some nice, fresh kooch!"

Big Ruby (with her rose tattoo and D.A. haircut) leapt onto the stage. She grabbed Rodney, the lead singer. Rodney's pubescent body trembled. Ruby whipped out her butcher-knife and, "whack!" Hacked off Rodney's nine-inch cock. Blood and gore overflowed. The crescendo played while Rodney screamed, "EEE AAAGGG EEE. My cock, my cock. How can I be leader of the Flesh Peckers without my cock!" He screamed with a gruesome cockney accent.

Ruby licked blood from the severed organ and smiled, "Don't worry, sweetie -- we'll have Doc Specimen sew you up a nice pussy."

"EEE AAAGGG EEE!!"

The Captain and his pirates lined up the women. They banged hole after hole. The Captain screwed two at once, using his ten-inch cock for one and his peg-leg dildo for the other. The pirates collected hair-pie souvenirs, "whack, whack, whack!"

The place was a screaming nightmare. "How can this be," David murmured in stunned confusion because he knew the pirates didn't belong. They were not part of this world -- they were not double-agents, Mek Men, or spies. This obscene intrusion must have been caused by a brain-hemorrhage or some mistake that slipped-in under the radar.

He watched Doc Specimen chop off thumbs and tongues. The violence and smell of blood were sickening. Everywhere, unbearable screaming. Everywhere, Jack Litch was taking shits. Ruby and the dykes were fighting the pirates for the stash of severed pussys. Hoary Fairy was playing with matches and kegs of dynamite. Was this the end? Would the alien die and write about his own funeral? Too soon! He hadn't found any answers -- he hadn't met the angel who was so enticingly close, but too far to reach. He knew they'd meet -- it was destiny (or was it). The alien was confused and in the grips of unrelenting anxiety and dread.

Gypsy cat leaped through the butchery. Cat paused for a short bath;

then urged the alien out of his stupefaction.   David followed the cat
through a camouflaged door.   He stroked the cat's fur in thanks,
momentarily distracted by the cacophony of an immense explosion as the
Celestial Orifice erupted in flames.   David realized he'd been very lucky
escaping from the clutches of a total mental breakdown or an untimely
death.   On several occasions an outside force ruled in his favor and
intervened at the most propitious moment to save him, but would his
luck continue?

~~~~~~~~~~~~~~~~~~~

V

CLOSE ENCOUNTERS

A gray cloud loomed in the sky like a vengeful deity. Entropic energy unwound, leaving nothing except silence. The end was always the same -- without substance. Yet, in that blind vacuum David was able to access his alien ability to reach back and recreate the past.

He wandered through wrecked streets, witness to the Final War, the "Mahabharata," a cosmic battle between the Rishis (god men) and the Nagas (serpent men). Humanity was caught between the opposing forces in a storm of total annihilation.

He was a simple merchant in Mohenjo Daro, a most prosperous city. The people lived in woven-towers spun from silver beneath glass pavilions. He saw the Vedanta war-machines and Vimana, the chariots that soared above the city like floating skulls firing explosive darts. Vessels (ten stories tall) descended from the stars and laid waste to his beloved city. A snow of burning silver fell upon the land. New diseases infected every form of life. Flowers and trees melted into monstrous apparitions. The oceans boiled.

David followed the gypsy cat through a worm-eaten door and found himself in an ancient graveyard. There were no electric lamps to displace the dark living-creature that could be felt, but not seen. It wrapped around David like a black fog with smoky talons. His third eye started to glow allowing David to cut through the blind density. He was standing in Death's Junkyard. Cement sepulchers were shattered as if bodies tore through the walls. Gravestones and monuments were overturned as if the dead had risen. Fear nibbled at the alien's composure. He lived in a world where life had no meaning -- it was only natural for the dead to exact vengeance.

"Help me." Voices rose from the ground, a cacophony of wretched pleas and unrelenting grief.

David was confused. He expected an angry mob of animated corpses trying to conquer the world, but the dead merely wanted to sleep undisturbed. An image of the Earth slipping off its axis blossomed in his alien-mind. It was that unfortunate event that caused untold consequences like waking the dead.

He followed the cat to a stone cavern and recognized the same cave he spotted through the keyhole in the Calabash Hotel. The appointed drop-spot was very close. The Numan waited within the cave. Cat scratched and whined, refusing to go any further. Alone again, David descended into crumbling catacombs and the remains of an ancient Gothic Cathedral. Balustrades and vaulted arches were carved into the rock. Everything was damp from underground seepage.

A large sarcophagus lay on a dais. Symbols along the sides indicated that it was a modern piece of equipment, a Time Vault. Through the window on the lid David saw the decayed corpse of a time traveler. The machine was invented to help dissenters escape from Magnumopolus. It never worked. Earth was frozen in time. People from other dimensions could be transported to Earth, but then they were imprisoned. David was able to travel the *time waves*, but he was always pulled back and never allowed to escape.

He descended into a lost realm, drifting back to a monastic world haunted by shimmering Gothic Images: gargoyles and Nephalem soared beneath vaulted ceilings that depicted heaven and hell. He drifted down a golden passageway through a crystal gallery and arrived at a misty grotto resplendent with radiant emeralds. David recognized a familiar aura beyond a pillar of stone and heard the cool, soft rustle of angel wings. "Hello, numb nuts." Lady Divine beamed.

He cursed to himself. What now? Were the Three Stooges about to drop from the ceiling and whack him on the head? David was pissed -- conned by reality or by the backhand of his cerebellum. David's alien senses were on high alert, but his exasperation waned when he saw Divine dissolve. It was a disguise. The illusion was replaced by a halo of feathery light and he recognized his contact slouching against a wall smoking a cigarette.

The angel -- lips smeared with red grease, silicon breasts poking through a tight sweater, false eyelashes fluttering in a pool of purple mascara.

There he was -- packed in plastic with tousled hair and defined pecs: angel, comrade, counterpart?

David's mumbling was a distraction. This was merely a spy game and he was here to exchange information. Once again, the image changed and he recognized an ordinary person in his twenties with traces of acne. He wore glasses, jeans, and a flower shirt that fell open to reveal a smooth, defined chest. Yes, the same boy David saw sacrificed on the altar in the church.

"Hey, dude -- got some grass?"

Certainly this was a signal, but David didn't know how to respond so he settled for the first words to come into his head, "I guess not."

"Well, that's ok -- why you down here, anyway? You're not a cop are you?"

"No, I'm no cop. I'm looking for information."

"What's that supposed to mean." The angel seemed defensive.

"You know, the revolution -- contact with the Underbelly."

"Look, man -- I'm a little high, but I don't know anything about no revolution. I've got a nice belly, though -- used to lift weights."

His contact was very coy. David needed to gain his trust so he revealed a little more about himself. "Don't worry, we can talk. I'm from the Outlands. I'm an alien."

"We're all aliens, man."

Now they were getting somewhere. There was no longer the necessity for codes. The angel told David about King Crimson, a rock-n-roll legend who recorded an album, *Twenty-Ninth Century Schizoid Man*. "That's me," he stated, "I'm from the future. Got these crazy powers like some kinda freak-angel, but I'm useless here. I'm stuck."

"I'm David Oblivion."

"Cool man. I'm Ken, but it doesn't matter -- I go by lots of names."

His words rushed out of him like water bursting from a dam, "Listen I'm pretty fucked up. Lots been happenin'. Been dealing for awhile to get some cash. Drugs man, not cool. Sold cars in L.A. Made lots of bread. Wanted a sex change operation. Crazy, hah? Wrecked a damn car, Buick Riviera. See -- there was this girl -- she can't get enough of me. That's cool. She came to L.A. I was crazy drunk. Pulled a kitchen knife on her -- scared myself -- pulling that kind of shit. She's not so bad, but hangs around all the time. We'd get stoned, drunk. I ended up in A.A. for awhile. Did lots of therapy shit. Right now, I'm pretty fucked up."

"Listen," David interrupted his flow, "we can help one another."

"I don't know -- you seem pretty messed up yourself. Like you got a stick up your butt."

"I can never be too careful. We've got to wear disguises, all of us."

"You sound like a spy. Maybe I could loosen you up. You could help me stay out of trouble. I need that. I still want that sex change."

"You're an androgyne. I'm alien. All part of the revolution."

"I don't know about revolutions, but I like to fuck -- just want to live one day at a time."

The rock walls seemed to pulsate with a penumbra of expectation. The angel was holding two crystals of liquid-light. He swallowed one and gave the other to David. The alien assumed the crystals contained relevant instructions. He swallowed the gift. They held one another while the crystals took effect, unraveling the skeins of vital information.

Reality began to shift. A symphony bubbled in David's mind. The earth collapsed and the stone grotto became a small island drifting among the stars. He became a rotating flux of identities transformed into a geyser of laughter, ripped apart, quartered and hung in sublime submission.

The angel unfurled his wings. His body glistened like silver snow melting into golden muscles. His eyes contained pools of swirling color, absorbing David in a world of silent wonder.

They smooched like kissing fish.

David touched the boy's cock with his mouth. He caressed the shaft with his fingers and encircled the head with his tongue. Down it slid into his throat. Sweet flesh jiggled in David's mouth. The cock was fragrant, like soap and honey -- balls were large, heavy weights that tasted like dried cum. The crack of his anus, just below the balls, was an aromatic confection. David was an excited alien tearing at his cumbersome clothes.

"My name is Lola," the Angel whispered, "I want you to fuck me."

"I am an Alien," David yelled, "I have tentacles and green flesh!"

"I am a woman and I like green flesh!"

They stood together -- naked, prone and ready for action. David was completely revealed. His green, gnarled belly hung like a paunchy gourd. His ruffled face, with three eyes and several rows of lips, blinked like a Christmas bulb. His hairless head expanded like a giant mushroom. Fifty tentacles extended from his body like the arms of a gigantic octopus. David's feet stuck to the floor like large suction-cups. His alien cock twanged like a purple cork on a spring. He was a heap of quivering, non-human flesh with one hell of an erection.

Lola lay on her back with her legs spread and her firm flesh smoldering. She removed her glasses and appeared transfixed by the alien who loomed and gasped before her. Her peach lips formed an exclamation point, "Oh, my!" She was hyperventilating. The alien wondered if she was excited or horrified.

Her penis was still hard. Cautiously David slid toward her. Tentatively he reached for her warm body. Delicately he touched her tender limbs with his outstretched tentacles. She moaned, "Yes, yes -- engulf me!"

Relief cascaded through David's nervous system as he enveloped her handsome body. He was ecstatic as he slithered across her torso, delirious with sexual abandon. She sighed, "I can love like a man and cum like a woman!"

David slid across her masculine chest and waved his purple prong in front of her eager mouth. He chided her into submission. When his ego was satisfied David fed his purple corkscrew into her deep throat. Electricity popped along his inverted backbone as Lola savored his alien sexuality. She artfully brought him to the peak of ecstasy without blowing his cork. She smacked her lips as David slipped out of her mouth and slithered across her golden-boy body. She trembled as he lifted her legs. He savored her anus -- probed the cavity with his flexuous tongue. The alien neatly parted the membranes with his serrated lips and wallowed in the hole. He secreted alien saliva while anticipating the "bang." He wavered like a monster above her prone anus.

David was quivering like a giant cock. He parted her cheeks. She moaned. He slipped his purple corker into the slot. Her eyes dilated as he probed with gentle force. David's skin was changing color from green to red. He was a torpedo, mercilessly penetrating a peaceful harbor. She thrashed with ecstasy and pain. He loved her as he deeply entered. Once inside, they shook and quaked together like dancing speed freaks. They moved in perfect harmony. Her ass was as talented as her mouth. David's brain screamed, "Give way, give way, give way."

He recalled making love for an eternity. One time, she-he fucked David and he split into a billion microcosms. David bounced around space like corn-kernels in an electric popper. He reassembled under the protective wing of his angel and they flew into the sun. It was free-fall love, tumbling like children. They got drunk, fell down and made love in the streets. It was always carnival time.

He was an athlete -- a beautiful man, a beautiful woman -- staring at David with a lopsided grin: half angelic, half stoned -- a cunning water-jaguar, a love-animal. They flew from island to star. He opened David and the alien was set free.

"Give way, give way," David's mind screamed as he pumped. The air churned with the heat of sex. He chugged like a hyperactive steam-engine. He fingered her charged nipples. She gasped as David enveloped her body with tentacles. He sucked her sacred flesh. They kissed and exploded. David's body escaped through his cock like a searing flame. Her cock jerked and shot hot rivers against David's belly. His lips burned with her touching and kissing. Her arms held him. He was cradled within billowing feathers -- angel wings. They were consumed with one another, protected within an effervescent bubble.

"Pop," the bubble burst. "Pop, pop." They were together in the stone grotto. "Pop." A TV-eye blinked. "Pop, pop." They were caught in a mind-trap, surrounded by agents from the Repulsion Bureau who stood like concrete columns with plastic facemasks. They carried laser rifles and radium shields. Caught. Completely revealed: an angel and an alien.

Alien Creatures Captured and Confined

Giant, green hulks sprayed the captives with hybrid-Jello. They were paralyzed, an angel and alien caught in the act of mind-swap love -- two frozen specimens. David was caught in the blob with his mouth open like a dying gargoyle. The angel was caught with one wing twisted and broken. Once the Jello hardened they were cut apart and separated. The cops loaded them in a patrol wagon that took them to the Repulsion Bureau. David was placed in a "process cubicle," a small white box that shot info-probes at his body. Strobe lights never stopped flashing. He was bombarded.

Probes dissected his chromosomes. Strobes pierced his mind and snatched vestiges of his personality. He was fed to a computer to be analyzed and digested.

Finally a guard retrieved David from the box and sprayed him with an emulsifier to melt his plastic encasement. David rebuilt his human camouflage. He still had his plunger and WIN charm. The guard placed him in solitary confinement, another white room.

David expected his prison cell to be a depressing tomb, but to his surprise it was quite comfortable. He had a soft bed, 3-D TV, and private bathroom with shower. A wall unit prepared three satisfying meals each day. The TV hung on the wall like a large oval-eye -- they watched each other intently. After five days David received his first visitor, a metal man.

The robot clamped David into his lap and whisked him away. The metal man sped through a nightmare of corridors on a cushion of air. David was deposited in the Hall of Control-and-Interrogation. He had been allowed to languish in reasonable comfort (no doubt, a tactic to lower his guard and soften him up for the kill). He was certain his interrogator would be Dr. Rubin S. Andros.

The room was empty except for two plastic chairs. David was in an immense cavern, a square mile of blank, white space. The door disappeared into the horizon. The floor and ceiling emitted a soft haze of light. He waited. Time seemed lost within the translucent glow and nothing happened. He sat in the plastic chair waiting for the Master Controller.

"Blink!"

Suddenly an image in a neat, white suit stood next to his chair.

"Hello, young man. I am Dr. Andros." His voice sounded indirect or pre-recorded.

"Are you a hologram or a living person?" David asked.

"I am reconstituted flesh -- very much alive! I am here merely to conduct some business. I'm a busy man, so please answer my questions quickly. I'm sure we will both be relieved when this interview is concluded.

"I might add that you have nothing to worry about. Also, there is no escape and your primitive weapon is useless. A protection-shield surrounds everything in this building. Now, before we begin, do you have any more obtuse questions?

Andros sat on the chair opposite David and smiled. He wore oval glasses and his eyeballs appeared to jiggle on springs behind the lenses. He was a small man with a shaved head and a goatee that appeared to be painted on his chin. David was sure Andros wanted to break down his defenses and make him confess (but to what?). He had to appear as cold and rational as his interrogator. "Yes, I have a question. What happened to the angel?"

"Angel? What are you referring to? Or are you trying to convince me that you are indeed crazy."

"The one in the grotto when we were arrested."

"Oh, yes -- the young hustler you were found grappling with. An unfortunate case. He was a venal addict, a schmecker. Fortunately we arrived in time. We actually saved his life. Of course we had to alter his features and insert a *tracker* in his brain. Still, I'm afraid we've lost him. He has slipped back to his old, self-destructive patterns. Here, I'll show you a recent hologram."

Andros retrieved a "flasher" from his pocket and projected a moving hologram. The angel looked ten years older and deformed. His clothes hung in shreds and his eyes were bloodshot and feverish. David watched as the angel crawled down a street, kicked and shoved by angry pedestrians. He told himself it was a false image created to undermine his confidence. David had to conceal his real emotions and appear strong.

Andros gloated, "Now it is time for me to ask questions and for you to respond. What is your true and complete name?"

"You know my name."

"Quite right -- that is an excellent answer. Indeed, we do know your name -- in fact, we know everything about you. We even have information that you don't know about yourself. Our computer is very thorough. Your genetic code reads like the Internet Comics and your brain is less than twenty gigabytes thick. You are almost as dull as your 'Journal.' So -- you want to save the world -- from whom, from what?"

David was beginning to panic -- what could he say? Words slowly came to mind and crossed his lips, "I think you are dangerous," but he couldn't rouse himself to say anything more.

"So, I'm the evil threat!" Andros laughed, "I'm merely an extension of the people. I give them what they want -- this is a democracy after all. You have the wrong impression of me. I'm an artist. I externalize monsters and make them harmless; in fact I wrap them in foil and sell them as luxuries. I give everyone the license to kill, but I make them pay. It's a nice arrangement, really. Society floats on the backwash of money. People buy freedom, which is a form of control. You're afraid only because you fear your own desires."

Andros was crawling inside David's guts like a serial killer. Maybe Andros was right. David could feel his whole act beginning to crumble, but he had to force himself to face his interrogator, "Why did you bring me here?"

"Ah, yes -- I was wondering when you would get to the point. You are here to be analyzed and judged. It is a matter of proper procedure -- life-and-death is always a matter of procedure."

"Am I on trial," David spoke hesitantly, "life and death?"

"You've already been tried. We are very efficient. Now it is simply a matter of procedure. You are here to answer one question: can you tell me something about yourself that I don't know, something the computer missed? Tell me anything that makes your life viable."

David felt the man's uncanny brain sitting behind his jiggling eyeballs, judging. It was as if Andros saw through the disguises and just wanted to see David squirm. He had no choice, David had to take his best shot, "I admit it -- I'm scared shitless, but what would it be like if this situation were reversed -- how would you react? What would you say to defend your life? Down deep, somewhere in your reconstituted flesh I think you are just as scared as me."

"Delightful . . . you truly believe in your own delusions. This will make an interesting article for the Psychiatric Review. But, I'm afraid you lose. Answering a question with another question is no answer at all. You will get your just desserts. Death, my boy. Death to you!" He laughed hysterically, then paused dramatically, "I love the effect my little drama produces in my subjects. I've always loved the theater.

"As I was saying -- I have no choice but to eliminate you. You are never satisfied. You are a social irritant, a malcontent -- and I will be better off without you. I'm selfish in that way -- I like to make my job as easy as possible. You couldn't begin to understand the responsibilities and demands that come with being the prime powerbroker in the world, The Controller. That's a little secret by the way -- most people don't know who makes the rules. They are content just bumbling along in their own little worlds and I like it that way. Enough chitchat. Death. Yes -- now that's a subject I can really get into.

"Specifically your death. In truth, and I've always been particular about telling the truth -- it is not quite as final as it sounds. I see your face light up with a spark of hope. Don't be too relieved just yet. You see, 'The Pits' are quite a lot worse than death.

"The Pits were built to contain the rubbish of society; rather like a giant dumpster," he said with relish. "David Oblivion, you are one lucky alien. You've won a free one-way ticket to The Pits."

Andros laughed as he plunged a hypodermic needle into his victim's arm. Eyes bulged, teeth glittered like fangs, and laughter splashed in David's mind as it dissolved into a nightmare. He became someone else, another person on another world.

◆◆◆ <u>The Masters</u> ◆◆◆

He was propelled through the void like an artificial satellite. There was a beacon in his brain. He was a human lighthouse tracking and diverting traffic through the emptiness of space; of course, it only seemed empty.   Time disclosed a congested universe, crowded with proto-forms and phantasms.

The function of the lighthouse-man was to operate like a computer in order to delineate the proper trajectories of passing debris. He monitored the navigation routes of all satellites in his sector.   It was a lonely occupation. He was cut off from all human contact. There was a digital scrambler implanted in his brain for work efficiency.   His form-cast space suit was his home. He worked without normal sleep. Rest was provided between computations. There was no time off, no vacations. His job would end when he physically broke down. He was stranded for life in the black hole of space. His only pleasure came from the dreams that ignited between the interminable lists of numerals.

He dreamt about emerald landscapes, billowing white sails rushing toward the edge of the world, colors splashing from pinwheels and slow-motion balloons caught within ripples of lazy music. He dreamt of chrome towers and spinning domes that floated above gleaming cities. Most of all he had dreams of people, dreams of Salene, his wild feline lover: Salene, cannabis, and music engaged in a ballet with gravity, roaming through the park on a long, peaceful day. Of course it wasn't like that -- reality is never like dreams.

His earth name was Ignatius. Everyone called him Ignuts. For a while he was a brilliant student; then during the "Epoch of Truth" and the breakdown that followed he became a junky. During that time most people who survived sought comfort in some form of addiction.

Ignuts' dreams turn into nightmares. He was a dead boy in his father's house.   He floated in saline solution and stank from formaldehyde. His father was a mortician, tall and lean, he spoke like a machine. Ignuts thought his father smelled like death, but that was only a fantasy. His name was Saul and Ignuts was never allowed to call him "father" or "dad." Saul always wore rubber gloves and a white, lab coat. He wore thick, round glasses that made his eyes bulge. Saul loved money. He often said, "People are worth more dead than alive." He rubbed his rubber-encased hands together and chuckled, "I'm in the perfect business to collect!"

Ignatius was an only child. He lived with his mother and Saul in a white house on Long Island. The family owned a Lincoln Continental,

Ford Thunderbird, and Mercury Montclair. Saul often pointed to the cars and informed Ignuts that he was a fortunate child. Saul loved cars. When he wasn't tinkering with corpses, he was playing with engines.

Ignuts' mother was not nearly as outgoing as Saul. In fact she was disturbed. She had a nervous condition and she twitched. Her skin itched and flaked because she was afflicted with Psoriasis. She had to cover her body with ointments and gels to stop the itching. She always appeared to shine like a ball of grease. Her name was Thelma. She was frightened of everything, and especially frightened of death. She was frightened of Saul because he was a mortician. She was afraid he would sneak up on her when she was sleeping and fill her with embalming fluid. She hadn't slept with Saul since the birth of Ignuts. They had separate bedrooms. Thelma was afraid of Ignatius because she never understood the relationship between sex and birth. She thought Ignuts was the spirit of a dead boy who came to haunt her because of Saul's sins. It only made sense to Thelma. She was always afraid. She protected herself by eating and watching television.

Ignuts watched his mother grow like a giant mushroom in a bed of fungus. Fat was her natural defense. She refused to leave her room. She grew solemnly before the glowing radiance of her television. The maid supplied Thelma with food, drugs, and other products that flashed across the TV screen. Saul was bored and frustrated with his wife. He often played with Ignatius to keep himself amused. Sometimes Saul tried to scare Ignuts to death.

Ignuts frowned as he stretched within the black universe of numerals and monsters. Digital read-outs spun through his mind. His brain burned. He smelled death.

He was eight years old again, in his father's workroom at the back of the mortuary. It looked like a kitchen. Everything was shinny and white made from chrome and porcelain. It smelled bad. A sheet was draped over a body on the metal table. Tubes filled with fluid disappeared into the corpse beneath the sheet. Ignatius was alone. He watched the sheet jerk. It jumped. The corpse sat up. Ignuts screamed. The dead face was like green putty. The boy was frozen in fear. A hand jerked and pointed at Ignatius. The boy fainted in terror. Then, he felt a hand shaking him awake and heard Saul's laughter. "Just a trick," Saul smiled. "The body is dead. The embalming fluid makes it move. It's an automatic reflex like a programmed machine, 'course I helped it along a little. Mustn't be afraid of the dead, boy, 'cause that's where we all end up."

Ignatius had to coordinate the list of predictions with course modifications. No time to dream. The joy he once experienced had to die forever. His feelings for his lost love could no longer continue. Sweet Salene, smooth as ivory on a bed of dark earth, no longer existed.

Ignatius noticed a reflection in the mechanical visor, all cracked and silent. He saw himself as a boy growing up. He wore thick, round glasses and his eyes appeared abnormally large like fish eyes. He recalled the corpse that sat up and pointed at him. He remembered a huge, greasy beast rising from a swamp. The beast devoured chocolate cherries, Hostess ding-dongs, Kaopectate, beer and pretzels. Ignatius watched momma eat. She never said a word. The television flickered and chattered. Saul was generous: he installed two new TVs in momma's room. Now she watched three programs at the same time: "Bowling for Dollars," "Search for Tomorrow" and "Lucy" reruns. Ignuts watched momma. He thought television was disgusting. Sometimes Saul watched the news on the big screen in the family room. Ignuts heard explosions, gunshots. Assassinations. War. He imagined bodies exploding. The television was killing people. Ignuts was frightened. He didn't want to be shot from behind without any warning. He started watching TV to protect himself.

Space is dark. Ignuts was fond of dark places. As a teenager he would hide beneath tables, under tablecloths; in basements, cellars, or dark attics. He would sit beneath blankets in rooms with drawn shades. He would sit without electric lights or candles. The only light came from the portable TV. Sometimes he listened to music on his I-pod while he watched TV. He pondered the symbolism in ancient Beatles' songs. He listened to Neo-punk and jerked off. The music was like razor blades. Ignuts thought about dead bodies and had an orgasm. Cum splattered the TV screen. Ignuts felt relief, he felt safe.

Salene was small and petite. Ignuts loved her in the dark caverns of his mind. She was like life-giving fluid. She revived Ignuts from the dead. He felt powerful with her because he could control her. She obliged his every desire. Salene was a fantasy. Salene was a corpse.

Ignatius met her one night in his father's workroom. He was seventeen. She was a fifteen-year-old victim of Leukemia. Ignuts was alone in the mortuary. He often worked nights when Saul wasn't around. When he met Salene she was covered with a sheet. He could tell she was beautiful. She looked like a holy statue beneath the white cloth.

Ignuts shut the lights in the workroom and lit a candle. Carefully he turned down the sheet and gazed upon the girl's lifeless body. She was too thin and an expression of pain distorted her face. It had not been an easy death. Nevertheless Ignuts was entranced. To him, she was a beautiful Sylph. He would paint her face and make it smile forever. He kissed her frozen lips and touched her stiff body. Slowly, as if under a magic spell, Ignuts stripped off his clothes. He stood naked before his princess. His penis was hard and swollen with desire. He climbed onto the metal table with the corpse. It was very difficult to penetrate Salene. She was very dry. He kissed her mouth. He used his hand to open her vagina. He used lubricant, but it was still difficult. Ignuts knew it wasn't her fault. She was trying to please him. She was very obedient. Ignuts kept Salene for two nights. It was his best memory. In the end he was forced to give her up for burial. Ignuts was never deluded to such an extreme that he believed her family could accept their love. Instead he imagined himself as Romeo torn from the arms of his Juliet. Salene was his first love and Ignuts was no longer a virgin.

Ignuts majored in mathematics at New York University. He wanted to build computers. He continued to watch TV for his own protection. He invented a direct hook-up, from the television to the brain. He was certain momma would enjoy the new device. Television poured directly into his brain. The screen was in the medulla oblongata. Thelma was too paranoid to try the hook-up. For a brief moment Ignuts was furious. He threatened her, but she only stuffed her mouth with Pringles and twitched. He realized there was no way to reach her. They were completely dead to one another and perhaps they always were.

Ignatius lived with two roommates, Creep and Snakelip. They were also students, but they were just filling time and space with no intention of getting a degree. They wanted to become musicians, to get rich and get laid. Their home was a dark warehouse on the lower east side. Everything was covered with foam rubber and painted black. A TV always flickered and a computer pumped out blasting sounds. Snakelip enjoyed beating Creep with a leather strap. Creep enjoyed the romance of crucifixion. Ignatius accepted the odd circumstances of living with Creep and Snakelip because they didn't have any expectations. The roommates never spoke to one another; instead they made noises or used signs. Ignuts preferred to speak in computer language. They initially became roommates because they shared a morbid curiosity about death, which was as strong as a painful toothache. Sometimes they had orgies in the cemetery with other students who didn't quite fit normal expectations. It was their idiosyncratic way to satisfy the human need to reach out to one another. Ignatius loved the cemetery.

Numbers click through his brain as he passes through time. He saw himself in the graveyard. Snakelip and Creep were there along with others from the university. They were celebrating the full moon with a "love-in" for the dead. An electric band cranked-out wails and screams, the sounds of the underworld. Everyone was stoned. Eyes dilated like pinwheels. Food and wine were shared. Their faces were streaked with paint and they wore luminous rags. Eyes and lips glistened in the moonlight as bodies turned, leaped, and dripped with sweat. A hawker sold hot dogs. The dancers waved florescent light-tubes that illuminated the cemetery like a meat locker in a supermarket. Ignuts sang like a banshee. He overturned gravestones and danced with the dead. Corpses greeted the living with open arms. Suddenly Ignuts saw metal containers fall from the sky. Neon saucers floated down like bloated maggots and he felt his stomach tremble and heave. A chill, like freezer burn, made his flesh crawl. A corpse pointed at Ignuts. Words fell from the hollow skull like hammer blows, "You are dead. We are all dead!"

Computations fill his mind. The lighthouse-man didn't want to remember. He merely wanted to stare into the infinite hole of space, but the hole was filled with monsters.

He remembered going home one rainy weekend where he could study in quiet. He read about experiments to alter the weather. He learned about the ecological breakdown caused by bombing the Middle East. He read about germ warfare, nuclear reactions, and military clones. The news was disturbing. Ignuts tried to immerse himself in computer language, which was purely rational with no emotional overtones. He didn't want to be afraid. Suddenly the television started to blink a new message. Microwaves were infiltrating his brain. The message screamed, "You are dead!"

Ignuts believed he was the only one who heard the messages and saw the UFOs. He observed people acting very strangely. Either they stared at him, or turned away in disgust. Sometimes strangers followed him. Inguts noticed people who looked like mutants hiding in dark alleys. He was certain he saw a man with a large, dorsal fin. One dark afternoon he saw a crowd of "fly people" crawling up the side of the Chrysler Building. He noticed people with bulging eyes that never blinked. Ignuts' imagination curdled. He wanted to be alone in the dark and hide. He turned off the reading lamp, but it got brighter. He pulled the plug from the socket but the light stayed on. He tried to turn off the TV, but it continued to flicker. Ignatius heard an unsettling sound, someone snickering, gloating over his discomfort. The stereo erupted. Sound shattered the room like a wrecking ball. The vacuum cleaner mounted an attack and the picture window exploded in an onslaught of glass knives. Everything yelled, "You are dead!" Ignuts knew the world was falling apart. The machines were rebelling. It was the beginning of the "Epoch of Truth."

Time and space collide within the brain of the lighthouse-man. Sometimes he cannot distinguish the dream from reality.

He remembered needles, drugs and war. Radiation ignited the world. Night became a luminous glow that crept into flesh and bones. Ovens exploded. Parasites ruled the streets. Everyone was hungry. Saul escaped in the Lincoln. He took a casket filled with money and a twelve-year-old nymph. Momma exploded in a flood of Pringles and Milk-of-Magnesia. Ignuts became a drug fiend, haunting abandoned hospitals, shooting smack and devouring pills. Creep and Snakelip tortured themselves to death.

Numbers expand and multiply in the dark space of his beacon brain. He tries to concentrate but instead he relives the past.

He remembers the pain. His body throbbed as if it was under attack by gangrene. He couldn't find a vein. He kept jabbing the spike into liquid flesh. Although his body hurt, he couldn't feel the prick of the needle or see the telltale trickle of blood. He was no longer hungry but his body was starving. Three days before, he stole a rat from a crazed kid – it was his last meal. He couldn't feel the dirt on his body, the fat lice and raw infections. Numb and naked, saliva foamed over his lips like a mad dog.

He lay on the floor of a warehouse and peered through a hole in the wall, watching the city. It shone like an iridescent wound. The sky bled through poisonous clouds. People crawled from their steel nests atop skyscrapers and climbed down to the streets. Some people dove from high pinnacles and crashed into the cement. The gathering crowd cheered. It was a celebration. They were wearing costumes, synthetic humps and enormous sex organs. Some celebrants were painted with blood. The Dragon Queen led a procession. She wore a display case from Tiffany's. The Halloween Ghoul hissed at the crowd. A group of Priests beat themselves with sticks and straps. The slapping rhythm provided the primal music for the gathering. Screams blended and rose like a choir of demons. He saw the hungry mob turn into a rampaging beast.

Suddenly lights flashed and the sky appeared to split. Ignuts saw enormous, mechanical locusts descend and hover above the crowd; vibrating with metal wings, turbines and computers. They were covered with rotting flesh harvested from corpses. They glowed with holy fire. They spoke with a voice that reverberated like thunder, "We are the Creators, the Masters -- You are The Dead. We invented you. We constructed you electron by electron. You are a simple machine programmed to cultivate and care for the Earth. You are a failed experiment, a machine that has gone insane. In error you developed an Ego. There is no ego, no individuality. There is no identity, no life. You are a machine! You have become a blight on Earth, an abomination in the Universe. You are dead! As the Creators we must intervene. We must render you harmless. We must take total control!"

Ignuts heard the thunder subside and was filled with a sense of peace. He was secure within the black hole of space where there was no fear or pain. He felt nothing. He still heard his father's laughter, but it no longer mattered.

VI
WHEN WORLDS COLLIDE

The sleeper descended one-hundred, forty-nine steps. The subterranean world was filled with peculiar aberrations. The weary traveler was stalked by a noxious vapor, a whispering fog that clawed at his mind with cries and laments, "we are disfigured souls. You venture into our world at your own risk." He could not escape the fog, but slid deeper into the miasma.

Two visages waited for the traveler like harbingers of ill repute: The Hanged Man and The Devil. They were alive, breathing icons transposed from the Tarot. The Hanged Man looked absurd, hanging up-side-down from the branch of a tree, yet he seemed at peace with himself and the world. The Devil squatted on a stone throne like an absurd parody, a beast-man with eagle claws, bat wings, and a goat's head with the ears of a donkey. A man and woman were chained to the throne. They appeared to be slaves, yet they could easily have escaped because the chains were not secured. The traveler was cornered. The Hanged Man was at his right, The Devil on the left, the insidious fog clutched his back, and an enormous boulder blocked his path. He needed to remove the boulder to escape from the subterranean world.

The traveler attempted to push the immense rock, but it wouldn't budge. The face of the boulder was the color of agony, deep black that forever fell into itself. The more he strained against the rock, the heavier it became. The Hanged Man swayed inviting the traveler to rest. The Devil offered unlimited power. The fog whipped his back with icy tendrils. The traveler reached inside himself for guidance. His mind grew calm -- muscles relaxed. Tensions dissolved. As the traveler relaxed the boulder began to move. Phantasms retreated. The boulder moved off the path, which opened into a cauldron of white light. The traveler was pitched forward through a rift in space and time.

❖❖❖ <u>The Pits</u> ❖❖❖

"Wake up . . . Come on, now!"

David's eyes popped open to harsh light and shadows. An ironclad cop hung over him like a giant locust. "Ordinance 451 states no one is allowed to sleep on the public beach. This is the second time I've caught you sleepin' off a hangover. This is it. If I catch you again I'm hauling your ass to jail. Get a room like a nice fella. Hotel Magnolia, up the street, always has vacancies. It's cheap. Now get lost."

He struggled to his feet and brushed sand from his clothes. "Where am I?"

"You must've been on some drunk. This is Venice Beach. Get going before I arrest you for being a public nuisance."

He moved off in the direction of the boardwalk feeling a little dazed, not knowing how he ended up on the beach. His face was rough with a week-old beard and sand stuck to his skin. Venice looked familiar as if he'd seen it in a dream. David could barely remember anything that occurred in recent weeks or months. He'd lost something, but forgot what.

He walked the beach and streets of Venice like an invader from another world. Once this place was a rich man's resort, a model of Venice, Italy -- now, a crumbling relic where outcasts and artists came to find sanctuary. On the horizon there were tall buildings, townhouses for the newly rich, part of the gentrification of America.

People were just beginning to wake up as the sun moved directly overhead. This was an older Venice, before the onslaught of vendors and tourists gawking at "freaks." Time seemed unstable, set in motion by a cosmic mistake, flowing from the past to replace the future. Buildings along the boardwalk looked like chunks of cake with pastel frosting melting in the sun. An amusement park appeared to waver in the rising heat like a ghost at the far end of the boardwalk, rising and sinking into the sand as insubstantial as a memory. Music drifted across the beach: jazz, ragas, rock. People wandered, lazily sat on park benches and gazed forever at the endless ocean. Old Jews sat near a synagogue, feeding pigeons and waiting for an Eternity. Ghosts everywhere. Several African Men pounded rhythms on Congo Drums while hippies danced to the beat.

David found enough money in his pockets to survive a week. He didn't care what happened after that. Nothing mattered. He was exhausted. He didn't want to live merely to survive -- forced to work at a crappy job just to live in a rat hole and eat junk food. David followed the cop's advice and rented a room at the Magnolia Hotel.

He searched the hallway for number ten. The door was open and someone was in the room, a black woman about forty. She was thin, worn looking, but still pretty wearing a dusty housedress with printed flowers.

"Is this room ten?"

"Yes, come in. I was just cleaning up. It isn't much, but it is clean. You look like you could use some cleaning up yourself. I'll bet you been sleepin' on tha beach and drinkin' your wine. Not that it is any of my business, but the bathroom and shower are five doors down the hall." Her voice was more friendly than critical.

"Do you work here?"

"I'm not one of the girls if that's what you mean -- not no more. I've better things to do with my time. But, I still help out round here. Small work, but I enjoy it."

"I'm not sure I understand."

"Honey, among other things, this hotel is what they used to call a 'cat house.' But, like I say, I'm no longer a working girl."

"Hey, sorry -- wasn't trying to lay a trip on you -- I'm just really tired."

"Yeah -- I can see that. Sit down in the chair. I'm almost finished.

My name is Teth Brown."

"I don't think I've heard a name like that before."

"Which name? Teth or Brown?" She laughed, "Just joking. My real name is Cessily, but kids called me Tethily because they couldn't pronounce it. I just shortened it to Teth -- much easier. Well, I'm finished here -- so what's your name?"

"I'm David, I think; although sometimes other names come to mind. Believe me I don't understand it myself. I've been walking for a very long time."

They had just met, but David felt he could trust her. He wanted to confide in someone, but mostly his mouth outran his brain. Self-pity spewed out like a hot shower and he ended by saying he'd hang on as long as his money held out, then it was all over for him.

Teth looked both concerned and angry. "Money is no way to measure life. You haven't lived long enough to know shit." With that she walked out and slammed the door.

The encounter left David drained and depressed. He lay down and fell into a deep and disturbing sleep. Snatches of dreams stayed in his mind. He saw someone jab a large needle into his arm; then he was in a dark place where his mind was bombarded by glowing numerals. There was another dream about a cave -- and an old Indian Woman who reminded David of Teth. She said people are all slaves, dominated by circumstances. So much was said, but he remembered very little -- just a few phrases, "Everyone is ignorant until they break the chain. Look for the miraculous in unexpected places. Open yourself." As far as he was concerned it was nonsense, but it left him feeling more at ease -- probably just the result of having slept.

It was evening when he awoke from his nap. David shaved and showered -- feeling much better he left the hotel to explore the beach like a tourist in a strange country. The sky exploded with streaks of violet, orange and red as the sun disappeared into the purple ocean. Like any tourist, he picked up a seashell and held it to his ear. Perhaps it was his overactive imagination, but it seemed as if the shell told a story.

Emperor Asoka of India lived thousands of years in the past. He began his reign as a warrior, but by the time he died he had become a pacifist. He wanted to protect humanity from the dangers caused by misusing science and magic. To that end the emperor established a secret group of nine adepts who were charged with the task of protecting knowledge. The adepts advanced the frontiers of science, but most of their discoveries were safely hidden.

David felt like a character in a cheesy, New Age film; sitting in the sand with a seashell attached to his ear like a weird phone, hearing stories about ancient India and "adepts." Worse yet, he was actually fascinated. He questioned his sanity. He was no longer certain where he was, or if he was even on Earth.

He went to a small restaurant on the boardwalk to eat dinner and then straight back to the Magnolia. He was still pretty exhausted -- couldn't keep his eyes open and quickly fell asleep. Bad dreams: slimy caverns filled with maniacs -- dripping fog trying to devour his mind. Then, the dreams were ablaze with radiant light and David awoke, grateful for the dawn.

He was eager to escape the phantoms of sleep and set out along the beach. Morning light exposed everything in high contrast like a photographic negative.

A young boy stood on the boardwalk -- tall and thin within an orange shirt that billowed in the breeze like a ruffled kite. Birds surrounded him. Pigeons perched on his outstretched arms. He was not feeding the birds, but they responded to his whispers. In the morning silence, the boy and his birds appeared to be meditating or praying. The scene frightened David and he quickly moved towards the beach. As he passed, David felt the boy's eyes penetrate his mind.

The beach was hazy -- a timeless desert. The ocean humped the shore like an animal caressing its' offspring.

A large limestone block rose out of the sand. David could discern a face in the rock. The illusion had the head and body of the Sphinx. The birth and death of the world was traced on the face of the enigmatic creature. He stood transfixed and became granite as the Sphinx acquired life and whispered secrets about a hidden chamber underground, a museum that contained records of past and future epochs -- a message from an Alien Civilization.

It seemed as though centuries passed in the presence of the Sphinx, but suddenly it faded and vanished. David was left feeling perplexed and hungry.

He felt better after breakfast and continued his journey roaming narrow back streets near the boardwalk. Splintered buildings stabbed the sky and he heard the distant refrain from an ancient rhyme about "London Bridges." He walked across shabby constructs over mud-choked canals. Tinker-toy houses crowded the banks of a trickling stream. The beach faded away into a fine, feathery mist that parted briefly to reveal a woman draped in shadows mumbling strange words and making signs with her hands. Her eyes were alive with visions -- her fingers wove an invisible tapestry. Living pictures flew before her hands: burning cities, rats, plague -- horses flying through the air carrying death. David saw an Empress shining like a star and wearing raiment spun from the sea. He was blinded by a fiery globe that whirled in space. Pushed off balance by visions, he fell into clouds of sand where sleep ensorcelled his mind for the rest of the afternoon.

After dinner David stood near the beach and admired the night sky. It shimmered like a web of tiny mirrors that reflected images frozen in time.

An old Rabbi stood in the doorway of a small Synagogue on the boardwalk. He wore a black skullcap. He had a bushy beard and wore a wool overcoat in spite of the summer heat. "I have something to say," he shouted as David walked nearby.

"We got a problem. Cockroaches. Nasty creatures. They are in the *Shul*. Everywhere. The bastards -- they are pretty smart!"

The little, old Rabbi told David an odd story, "At one time cockroaches were probably as large as humans. They may have been the first intelligent creatures. There is evidence that indicates they made machines, built cities, and created art and science." He started to rock back and forth mumbling prayers, then looked at David and continued his account. "Even millions of years ago, they were filthy creatures -- instinctive scavengers. They produced great quantities of garbage and lived in it -- as a result they lost intelligence and became small, nasty pests.

"So now I know that humans are not at the top of the heap. I worry that God is a cockroach." The Rabbi bowed his head, mumbled more prayers and walked back inside the Synagogue.

In an alley off the boardwalk David noticed a light in the window of a small shop. Red letters on the sign above the door announced, "Krapes Emporium." He thought there might be something familiar in the shop to bring him back to reality. So far whatever he experienced seemed so bizarre that he felt lost in a mad man's dream.

Everything inside was covered in layers of dust. Glass cases crowded the floor leaving very little room to maneuver. In one corner there was a metal grate beneath a sign that said "pawnbroker." David felt slightly reassured by the apparent normalcy of the place, but the more he looked at objects behind the glass the more his reassurance disappeared. Some items were labeled -- he saw "unicorn horn" and "dragon wing." There were small black-cubes labeled *egglets* and glowing objects identified as *oospheres*. He noticed several large jars under a sign that read "glandular conditions." He was relieved because the glass on the jars was so discolored and cloudy he couldn't make out the contents. A tall purple crate stood in a cage near the back of the shop with a sign that read "Martian Mummy."

David was about to leave when he was accosted by Captain Crunch -- at least it sounded like the cartoon spokesman for the cereal by the same name. "How goes it, matey m'boy."

David turned back and saw a cadaverous man in a red-striped jacket, wearing black lipstick and an Andy Warhol wig. He was smiling. There was a bad taste in David's mouth, "I was just about to leave."

"Nay, matey -- stay. I'll show you some wonders. Perchance we can strike a deal. What's your pleasure?"

"Just looking -- really. I need to get back to my room."

"No fun in that. Perhaps you have something to sell. I'm a pawnbroker -- best in town. Of course I only handle unusual items. If you have an ordinary ring to sell I don't want it, but if you have a 'power ring' I'm your man. I pay the highest prices anywhere. Let me show you some of my precious cargo."

"Not really interested in selling or buying anything."

"Don't be a spoil sport, m'boy. Come along."

David found himself drawn toward the smiling cadaver as he wove his spell.

"That's it lad. This way. I deal in Neoteric Dimensions. I sell a preparation called 'mental slop' -- you might be interested. It is guaranteed to grow hair follicles inside the brain -- quite an extraordinary experience. I keep a regular stock of *Loomies*, but sometimes I run out of *Draco Nins*. I personally authorize all virgin births in the area. I have a large collection of poly-globular eyeballs. Right this way. For a small price, I sell glimpses of the future -- invariably accurate. Well, matey is there anything I can temp you with?"

David's stomach was doing flip-flops. He was convinced that none of it was real, but didn't know how to escape. "I have everything I need . . . Just want to get back."

"Going somewhere so soon. We've hardly had time to get acquainted. Let me give you a parting gift to show there are no hard feelings."

The cadaver handed David a stone.

"What's this?"

"Don't worry dear boy -- it won't bite. It's the eye of a *Venusian Swort*. The creature died in the arms of an astronaut -- a tragic love affair. The astronaut sold the eye to me in prostrate destitution. Stare at it -- it will help you see."

Nothing happened when David looked at the stone, but when he looked up he was on the street outside the shop.

After another night of incomprehensible dreams he woke to his third day in Venice. Some inexplicable urgency pushed him out the door across the ancient plain of sand that was once the bottom of the ocean. A large monolith stood beyond the abandoned pier. David struggled across the sand as if climbing an enormous mountain. The monolith was a stone gate decorated with pictograms and peculiar symbols.

The Gate of the Sun at Tiahuanaco stands thirteen thousand feet above sea level in the mountains of Bolivia, carved from a ten-ton boulder.

An ornamental frieze on the gate depicts birdmen with webbed fingers that seem to operate mechanical vehicles. When some of the symbols were deciphered, an accurate calendar for the planet Venus was revealed. No one knows the age of the gate, thousands or millions of years old. The gate leads into a monumental city in ruins. The Indians believe the restored city continues to survive deep underground.

As David stared at the gate, stories and visions raced through his mind. He witnessed the first Man-Woman burst from a star seed and generate the Primal Civilization. Humanity divided -- separate cultures developed. The Primal Knowledge was distorted and lost in a flood of dying civilizations. The writing on the gate indicated that some of the early knowledge was still preserved in an area known as "Terra Prohibida" beyond the Rhio Xingu, a tributary of the Amazon. Explorers have searched for hundreds of years for a lost city in the jungle to no avail. Everyone who has attempted the search has vanished. A rumor claimed the whole universe floated in a silver pond at the heart of the lost city.

David found himself wandering on the promenade not knowing how he got there. Vague images flashed in his mind that made no sense, but filled him with a sense of awe and great expectation.

The afternoon stretched before David like a blank page. He stopped for a late breakfast and noticed how extraordinary everything tasted. After leaving the café he proceeded to explore the narrow streets off the main promenade. Small cottages were separated by gardens and trellises along winding pathways like a village in a storybook. David watched a woman with white hair wearing a patchwork-dress kneeling in her garden, tending her flowers. He heard a chorus of tiny bells as her old hands encouraged the garden to grow. David swore under his breath -- before his eyes the flowers reached for the woman's hands and burst into brilliant colors. The improbable was becoming commonplace. David sought refuge back at the hotel and spent the rest of the day in a state of semi-consciousness.

It was dark before he ventured out again. He planned to stop at a grocery store for some food to take back to the hotel room, but he was waylaid by a portly, young man dressed in a dark suit carrying a briefcase.

"Look," he addressed David, "the sky is expectant."

"What?"

"We must address ourselves to the sky. The Guardians of Time inhabit the sky!"

Why me David thought, but replied, "sky's empty." It was the wrong thing to say because it set the man off. He began to ramble and rant about stars, artificial satellites and other objects that can't be seen by the human eye, but are always there, hanging like overripe fruit pregnant with potential about to burst forth with quotidian revelations and catastrophic consequences.

"They exist," he shouted. "UFOs. Angels. I've seen them, the Elohim! They exist to keep balance in the universe."

It was as if he was on some sort of speed. He talked about an intergalactic war involving Ormazd and Ahriman, ancient deities, *aliens* who represented "light" and "darkness."

"They wage war over the control of Earth. Winner takes all. The *Grays* are part of it. They're mercenaries who abduct humans and turn them into mindless soldiers or use them for breeding stock."

David tried walking away but he was followed down the boardwalk. The man talked incessantly. "War on earth, misery and death -- all caused by the intergalactic conflict. As above so below. Earth is a reflection. The Elohim are seeking recruits to help them keep balance. Time is beginning to crumble. Skies are pregnant with visions. Information packets are dropping from heaven. We must search the skies. Open your mind -- let them in!"

The man was shouting at the sky and gesticulating. David's brain was on overload -- he was frazzled, but could that explain the dim outline he saw hanging in the sky like a golden goblet? A beam of light traveled from the goblet to the young man's solar plexus. Pictures and symbols flowed along the beam and the man in the dark suit disintegrated in plain sight.

Daybreak rescued David from his bedevilment. He could face the light, besides he was hungry and that was incentive enough to leave his room.

Each day he walked further through what seemed to be dissolving spaces between the sun and sand. He arrived beneath a distant pier strolling among columns of wood and stone, deeper into the gloom through a world of fallen pillars and haunting shadows. Deep in the recesses he saw a chamber of light where the sun had broken through a hole in the timber ceiling. A glowing city emerged from the gloom. It was called Agartha -- a holy citadel planted on Earth to protect the history and knowledge of the universe. Time was recorded on reels of light and kept in the sacred library. David saw volumes of information stored in crystals. Actual events were recorded as "glyphs," pictures charged with vital energy. Every bit of information was alive. David was bathed in arcane wisdom. His brain spun like a cyclotron, synthesizing new knowledge. The rush was too much . . . David's mind split -- overloaded. Fine glass shattered. He could no longer understand. Everything was forgotten. The chamber grew dark. Agartha was lost.

David stumbled over wooden beams searching for an exit. Shadows of people or deformed creatures hid beneath the pier. Small sunspots danced in the dark like sparks. The spots grew large becoming snapshots, windows cut into the darkness, cameos of the beach and ocean. The boardwalk came into view like a stage after the curtain rises.

Life was a riot of color and movement. Hippies played drums and danced. Bodies lay on the beach like perch in a frying pan. Old ladies sat on benches and gossiped in Yiddish. David turned down a street built on top of a canal filled over with cement and bricks. All the houses were ambushed by weeds and wild flowers like a slum in a fairy tale.

A girl with red hair danced on the pavement like a bird with wild feathers, rhinestones, and colored skirts. Red and purple patterns were painted on her face. She danced in easy circles that broke into leaping and jumping like a jittery parrot caught in the wind. Music dripped into his mind as the girl blithely unwound. He heard sounds that were joyful and sad, unearthly music generated by her dancing mind. David was captivated, slowly absorbed into another world. He felt himself take flight and glide into the perfect sound.

When he returned the street was empty. The sun slipped over the edge of the horizon and the flaming bowl of sky was extinguished by the night.

He bought a hot dog and chips, sat on a bench and watched the night dissolve into fog.

"Howdy son," a voice came out of the fog which parted to reveal an old woman with a bottle of wine.

David stammered a cautious greeting. He didn't know what to expect from the unexpected.

"Son, Pull your seat over and have a sip of wine -- I got news." The words came out in one long, sloppy slur. She wore a tattered coat --

newspapers and pamphlets overflowed from oversized pockets. Nylons draped over her brown boots. A green hat with plastic daisies sat on a rat's nest of gray hair. She looked very drunk. David wisely refused her offer of wine.

"How ya been -- I don't really care," she mumbled. "I'm Marla. Some folks say I'm crazy. Not important anyway. I tell this story -- same story -- over and over. Same thing but no one remembers. So I keep tellin' it." She rambled on, talking more to herself than to anyone else.

At one time she was a lay minister who worked for some Evangelical Preacher, but all that ended when she became pregnant with his baby. Being an upstanding leader of the church with a wife and two small children, the preacher refused to stand by Marla and his unborn child. Instead she was forced out of the church by rumors and innuendos. She suffered a miscarriage and started living on the street.

She repeated the story and the more she drank, the stranger her story became with biblical references and religious connotations. "Jesus came from the stars. To teach us. The Star of Bethlehem -- Ezekiel's Wheel -- a UFO bringing news of the holy birth. Like me . . . Mary was visited by an angel, an alien-astronaut who planted the seed."

She became agitated and talked about Jesus Christ as if she personally knew him. "He was a rebel. He had a higher calling. No one understood. He wandered in the desert and met the Star People. They took him to a cave near the Red Sea where he learned the True Knowledge. When he returned, he was a joyful man. His message was simple, 'Enjoy life. Help one another. Do your best.'"

She began to change as she talked. Her story was bizarre but her demeanor was reverential -- the alcohol no longer had an effect. "They tried to crucify Jesus, but he didn't stay for the occasion. Instead he hosted a beggar's banquet. He drank and danced in the street. He made love to Judas and Mary Magdalene. He got high on the night they nailed him to the cross. He escaped in a silver UFO. People were not ready. Still not ready. People too scared. It's all about money. Fear and money. The story doesn't change -- Krishna, Mohammed, Buddha. It doesn't change. People just want the big death. Waiting for Armageddon. Messiahs come and go. They're a dime a dozen. I hear we got a new one right here in this pit of a town."

Marla finally ran out of words and silence filled the emptiness. The fog receded giving way to a dark night with no stars.

Nightmares pursued David as soon as his head hit the pillow. He was on an island floating in space. War raged around him.

~~~~~~~~~~~~~~~~

VII
CROSSING THE THRESHOLD

A knock woke David. He struggled into his pants and opened the door. It was Teth.

"Hope I didn't disturb you -- it's past twelve. I work today and wanted to stop by and apologize. I get angry sometimes when it's really none of my business."

"Thanks -- but you were probably right to lay into me. I was acting pretty lame."

"We all have bad days."

"You said it's after twelve. Can't believe it -- I'm usually up by 6 a.m. -- been seeing some pretty weird stuff."

"I'll be the first to admit if something's weird it'll end up here."

"Why is that?"

"Not sure. Maybe it's the vibes around here. You still thinking about suicide?

"Haven't thought about it in awhile -- been too busy checking out all the weirdness."

"I always say, 'weird' is good for whatever ails you." They both smiled.

Teth talked a little about herself -- said she hadn't thought about suicide in years, but it was still a sore spot. One day she realized she had a choice. The idea that she could take her own life gave her a sense of control and she knew she could also choose to live.

"You like parties," she asked. David nodded. "There's one at the Gashouse, tonight -- the building with the painted dove above the entrance. Come around nine. Maybe I'll see you there."

The rest of the day faded like stills from an old motion picture turning dark with age. Beads of mist reflected the moon as night settled like a black cape over the beach and promenade.

The building was a crumbling facade with an attached colonnade. The walls were painted white and appeared to glow with the reflected light from a three-quarter moon. The place was boarded up, but a flap of wood partially covered a broken door that served as an entrance.

The inside of the Gashouse was dark and musty. A bathtub with claw-feet stood in the middle of the floor. A naked man sat in the tub and read a poem. Some sort of stage was behind the tub, closed off by a wall of curtains. There were a few old couches and lots of tables of various sizes with wooden chairs occupied by beatniks who were absorbed in the mellow sounds of jazz that floated through the room. The black walls were covered with protest art. Several anti-war sculptures stood around the room like pieces of collateral damage.

Hippies arrived later -- dressed in tie-dyed clothes, listening to Bob Dylan and Mick Jagger -- exchanging flowers and food. Everyone began to dance. The place became a kaleidoscope of colorful reflections.

The sound of a pipe organ intruded with *Amazing Grace* and the dusty curtains at the back of the room were pulled up to the ceiling like seagulls yanked into the sky. More curtains and drapes were opened to reveal a spectacle: a gold foil Stairway to Heaven surrounded by pink, crepe clouds. A painting of Judy Canova (star of 1940s comedies) wistfully hung from a star in a painted sky. The giant staircase slowly turned like a spiral corkscrew drilling a hole through the starry ceiling. David was completely absorbed by the freeform dazzle and glitz.

A purple lizard dressed as a Ring Master stood in front of the staircase and eulogized, "Welcome everyone. Welcome to the parade of history."

People in fantastic costumes posed on the revolving staircase. One man was dressed like the Roman Coliseum complete with Christians being fed to the lions. Someone was dressed like the Great Pyramid of Cheops. Every costume was an outrageous miracle or an obscene drama. The Hanging Gardens of Babylon swung back and forth to *Steam Heat* sung by Peggy Lee. The Tower of Babel crumbled like a skyscraper in an earthquake.

Groucho Marx chased Lady Astor through the mayhem. The giant heads of Easter Island nodded and smiled. Menhirs and dolmens sang *That Old Black Magic* in the middle of Stonehenge. David's mind was playing tricks -- he was confused by lavish elaborations.

"Confusion often leads to illumination," quoth the ravine -- the ravenous ravine that devoured the immortal liver of Prometheus. Confusion gave way to the Three Stooges performing Bertolt Brecht -- gave way to Judy Canova who split atoms with her horse laugh. She rose above the confusion like a crescendo. Everything else was just confetti.

The room grew dim and quiet. Lights flickered below the level of perception transforming the walls and floor into glowing lace. Space shifted into a cave of living fiber. David lay cradled on the gently vibrating floor.

He was drawn to a few people sitting on a hill overlooking a central garden. As the spaces in the room converged he found himself next to the group. He was offered wine that exploded on his tongue causing bubbles to collide in his brain. Invisible fingers plucked his ribs like a harp. David's backbone slipped and shimmied like a nervous snake. A clown cavorted in the garden and he couldn't stop laughing.

He fell into a psychedelic daydream. It was opening night for an elaborate stage-play written in some backroom within his mind. The characters were familiar. Teth was the clown surrounded by the people he encountered on his journey: the boy with silver eyes, the shopkeeper, the old woman -- all of them shifted in the light -- emerging from a cave by the Red Sea: nine Adepts preserving the knowledge of the world.

The clown wore a blue jester's cap with bells. She looked over at

David, "Glad you could make it."   In that moment, pieces of an unsolvable puzzle clicked into place.   Through the clash of colors, jangling sounds, and improbable encounters David discovered the Underbelly. It was right where he sat.

A great deal of information was decoded.

(The brain is merely a computer -- a memory bank programmed with tendencies and habits. The Mind exists as a process beyond the physical equipment. The Mind is the transmutation of energy)

Teth told him about Jubilant Technologies and Paradise, Inc.: new paradigms implemented to create a working harmony between nature and human invention.   Total Systems used hybrid components linked together for greater efficiency and the conservation of overall energy. She said, "We must remember we come from the Earth. The goal is to restore Balance."

David's senses tumbled over one another. Dark clouds moved across the sky and blotted out the lights. Someone whispered, "Tell him about the Alien."

He sat in the back row of a tiny theater and watched an amateur production of _The Tempest_ by Shakespeare performed as a science-fiction musical. The familiar characters were transformed into slapstick parodies. Calaban was an alien-monster. Prospero wore a space helmet. Ariel was a hermaphrodite with angel wings.

A voice intoned, "The alien wanders from one world to another, forever haunted and alone. The alien is within everyone feeding on fear."

Another voice spoke, "I am also an alien. I stared into the Dark and I saw Light. My vision was unflinching." Ariel's wings unfurled and the angel took flight.

Prospero advanced to center stage. "The alien must be recognized before we are allowed to emerge from the cage of brute survival."

A Greek Chorus stood behind Prospero and chanted, "The relationship between birth, death, and rebirth provides the key."

Prospero intoned, "Understanding cycles has always been the way to achieve harmony with elemental forces."

A booming voice from the sky exclaimed, "The human body is a vehicle that takes us through a three-dimensional existence. The Earth is a vehicle that takes us through a multi-dimensional universe."

All the actors came on stage and sang a rollicking song, "Down on your heels, up on your toes -- stay after school, learn how it goes. Everybody do the Varsity Drag."

The theater faded like fireworks against a black sky. Fireflies danced in the dark. David dreamt about aliens.

The Earth trembled. The ceiling of the cave was transformed by the Aurora Borealis. The lights spoke, "Time recurs along an infinite spiral. Civilizations have risen only to fall. Homo-sapiens are an endangered species. There are Guardians, but people are blind to Angels so they falter."

A single spotlight was lit. The center ring was bathed in gold and the clown stepped into the light. She raised her hands to disclose four balls: black, red, yellow, and white. Teth spoke as she juggled, "The universe spins within a dichotomy of opposing-forces. The juggler constantly plays with extremes: gravity and momentum, various weights, energy and torque. An Adept learns to perform a precarious balancing act like the juggler. Every performance occurs in the mind, the bridge to the universe. When the Adept crosses the bridge he-or-she becomes a Numan."

A circus band began to play. Clowns, trapeze artists, and daredevils trotted into the ring. Loudspeakers rang with the voice of the Big Top, "Ladies and gentlemen, the Turtle Constellation shines above New Jerusalem ushering in a new Golden Age. The Greatest Show on Earth is about to begin. The Adepts will seed the planet with new thought-forms and manifestations. You will witness the return of Angels."

Teth turned toward David, "It's time to get started. I am about to play Program Number Ten. If you accept the program it will put you on the chosen path."

She turned the crank on an antique, Edison Gramophone and put a wax cylinder on the spool. A movie screen was placed in the middle of the floor. A reel of film was threaded through an old movie-projector. The machine was turned on. Light flickered on the screen and he stared at an image of himself, "Hello David Oblivion, this is Program Number Ten."

His mind went blank (brain freeze). Everything turned white. He heard a voice in his head, "The working organization of life begins with the Hebrew Letter Teth which symbolizes serpent-power. Teth is the principle force that sets life in motion."

David was on the screen, in the movie. The first several months of the program revealed many painful struggles. Slowly a change took place. Pain gave way to energy. He felt the growth of inner strength. Teth (Prana) entered his body on vibrating wings.

A recorded voice imparted more information, "The big questions about life and death are rarely discussed. Society is at variance with non-conformity. The individual is subjected to indoctrination and electronic conditioning."

The Adepts were remaking the world, but David had to start with himself. The voice-over from the gramophone continued, "A person changes as his/her images change. People are transformed through symbolic vibrations: words, paintings, music, and sculpture. The mind is tuned by symbols."

David was discovering his authentic self.

The movie spilled color across the walls and floor. Music got up and danced, "Boogie, boogie down, baby." The Marx Brothers jumped off the screen. Kingdom-come embraced May-hem. David's brain became an illusion -- he was alone in a room that existed in a clock. The red second-hand stopped. Time melted on a shelf. He was caught between the hands of the clock -- stopped, with no escape. His brain erupted in flames that caused an explosion. A junk man picked up the pieces and stuffed them in a canvas sack. Inside the bag, David was greeted by the boy with silver eyes. He talked like a bird. He whispered a prayer in David's ear. They made love. Silver eyes splashed like confetti. The movie crawled back into the screen.

He was entranced. Teth's naked body glistened like polished bronze. Her body felt like liquid slipping from hard to soft. David's blood was charged with urgency. It was easy -- like resting on the back of a giant Condor -- floating -- sailing on the wind -- slipping from hard to soft, simply enjoying the pleasure.

Program Ten spoke from the screen, "So much human effort is wasted on suffering. Laughter is a better alternative."

David watched the movie blast-off with a flourish of activity. The

Adepts were creating a circus-tent from red-flannel rags. David painted clowns and elephants on the walls of the tent.

They were new world crusaders panhandling for Paradise. They planted seeds of dissent. They baptized people in pure Light, Enlightenment. Circles were formed to heal the world.

Images swam across the movie screen. The Earth Chrysalis was waxing in silver radiance. Humanity was building a launching pad. A gleaming ship rested in the brazier of early dawn.

"Click," the recording stuttered, "Time to wake up. Program Ten is complete. You are a Numan. Welcome to the Circle. Click."

David found himself in an unfamiliar room, but he felt comfortable and serene. He recognized Teth and the other Adepts.

"What happened? Am I still in the movie?" He asked the group.

It was Teth who answered, "The movie ended awhile ago. You've been living with us for the last four years."

Memories whirled in David's mind like stallions on a carousel. He remembered everything and felt changed: he was no longer defined by fear.

"Will you stay with us? Or, do you wish to leave?"

He wasn't quite ready for all that had occurred. There were still doubts. It seemed too beautiful, too "new age," but he couldn't deny the voice he heard within himself. "How can I leave? There is nowhere else to go."

"You are the tenth -- the number necessary to complete our Great Work. We have been constructing an Arc of Light to take us to the stars. It is time to greet the Alien."

He wondered if he'd heard wrong -- was this a mistake? Were they about to drink the Koolaid? David saw the Arc of Light in his mind, a manifestation, a "mind ship." He realized these people cared for him. He trusted them. This was not *Heaven's Gate*, the cult that would dominate the headlines in an alternate future. This was the Underbelly and together they were Numan.

<u>The Trip into Space and Beyond</u>

Noise rumbled through the room like junk clattering in metal cans. Everyone shimmied as the rumble eased into bright, snappy melodies played on brass horns and saxophones. The melodies shifted into electric-guitar serenades. They all clicked heels and danced. The serenades slid into violin concertos and etudes. Indian Ragas dribbled down atonal scales. The music became a Sound, a Tone, and a volcano of Living Color.

David heard a voice exclaim, "The line of syzygy is our path to the universe. The Mind is our vehicle. We are propelled by Intention."

The room disappeared. A Mind-Ship formed above the group like a vermillion skull floating in the ether, enveloped by a golden sail of ionized light. Slowly they rose from the solid earth and ascended into the chamber of the skull. The ship shifted and soared -- stretched beyond the sky.

Altered Spaces

Billions of candlelights pierced black infinity. They soared into the crest of searing night. The skull-ship glowed deep and red with eyes that were hollow cutouts shaped like night birds. The black of space enveloped David's mind -- he was eclipsed and alone -- remembering. Everything flowed back: the city, the wars, the damage and loss. He remembered, "I am David Oblivion -- an alien. I am searching for my counterpart, my split half."

He lost his mind and soared like an Angel. The planets were stepping-stones. The Sentinels of Dark and Light harmonized *Three Blind Mice* while they waged an eternal clockwork-war. A crippled Jesus hobbled across the Yellow Brick Road with an old man tucked under his arm.

Giant cockroaches invaded Galaxy "X" led by Mrs. Homily waving a dead chicken and plastic crucifix. In the torrid swamps of Saturn Reverend Kinship led his crusade of expurgation. Leona the Domina leered at David from a cloud of methane gas.

The universe was in motion. A comet blazed a hole through space. Lady Divine rode on the fiery head. The sex pirates attacked Galaxy Number Nine. Yama the insatiable God of Death cut down the pirates. The swollen skull-ship split -- the explosion eclipsed David's reflection. He sank into the depths.

He heard the plaintive call of barren worlds, alien horizons -- they called with the voice of a bereaved lover.

He passed through storms, pitfalls, and flaming whirlpools -- through the gulf of infinity. He flew beyond the spectrum of known light and shattered against the wall of impenetrable sound. He splashed like an atom against the Source: "Ruach Elohim" / Center / World / Cosmic Dance / Radiating Eye -- The Alien. David Oblivion burst. The sound was too bright. The energy -- too strong. The face was too benevolent. Lights flickered. The face! The face of Dr. Rubin S. Andros!

No Deposit - No Return

Struggling out of the pit, David felt like a casualty of war -- realizing he was back at the party before the invasion, still waiting for the comet Kohoutek. Nothing changed. People danced. Ken (the angel?) was serving drinks.

"Ken. Man -- I thought I'd lost you."

"Nah. I'm just doin' my thing. Hey, you're not mad? I mean we didn't really hit it off. I'm ok with it -- so long as we stay friends."

"oh, yeah -- sure. It's ok."

David didn't really understand, but he played along. There was a particular logic to the way events in his life unfolded -- as if he kept meeting the same people, only they wore different disguises and David kept making the same mistakes.

He wandered around like a lost alien until he spotted an older man who looked vaguely familiar, standing in the corner bathed beneath the red glow of a disco ball. "Hello," the man spoke as David moved in his direction.

"Have we met?"

"It's possible, but I'm just a tourist. Here on a short vacation."

"Where you from?" David asked trying to figure out how he knew him.

"I used to live in the city, but I moved a very long time ago. Now that you mention it, you also look familiar."

Recognition dawned on David with blunt finality. "It's you isn't it!"

A small smile creased the man's face like a crack on the shell of an egg. He nodded. It didn't make sense. How could this old man be Dr. Rubin S. Andros?

"The last time we met you were very upset with me. I can't say I blame you. I was acting like a pompous dictator. As you can see I've aged some -- maybe gotten smarter."

David was baffled. "Was any of it real? What about the Adepts? The Numan? What happened?"

"Oh -- it was real alright, but not in the way you might think. This has all been a record of your life. I'm you and you are me."

As soon as the words left his lips David knew they were true, but he couldn't accept the reality. "How is it possible?" David was filled with anguish. He faced himself: a person he despised.

Andros solemnly replied, "I know exactly how you feel. But I did help in the end. I sent you to the Underbelly -- that's what you wanted. Besides, we've met like this before. I was a lot younger. You called me an invader, a monster, etc., etc. You were about to murder me, but you realized I am your split-half. We are one person. You were paralyzed with indecision. I've come back to end this now, one way or another."

David remembered: he stood over his nemesis with his prone weapon (a plunger?). It was a precarious position. If David struck, he would be killing himself. "You're different -- older. What happened?"

"I relented. I accepted my mortality -- my imperfections. I was much more capable of living in the world than you so that's what I did. Just like everyone else -- I got a job and paid taxes. I stopped painting. Stopped writing or doing anything creative -- all that was *you* anyway. I became a workaholic -- that's all I did until I retired. Now I sit around and wait for the day when they plant me in the ground. That's why I'm back; I've got nothing else to do."

He was David's enemy, but he was also his split half, the same person. "I won't kill you, but I can't accept you like a long lost buddy. You're still the controlling bastard who doesn't give a shit about anyone but yourself."

"True. So what's the answer? I don't want to be left hanging for the rest of my life. Kill me if you want, but we're both dead then -- and I don't think you're ready to die."

In the end they both agreed. Andros stayed and David left. It was a pretty good solution. Andros got to act out his megalomaniac delusions, stuck in the nineteen-seventies; and David Oblivion resumed the life

Andros was leading in the new millennium.

David now lives in a retirement community in Palm Springs, California. He is exploring creativity while searching the skies for unusual phenomena. He knows the Adepts exist and he is tracking the evolution of Numan. Angels are just beyond his peripheral vision. He continues to warn people about Magnumopolus and the threats posed by Zeitgeist. David's doctor says he is completely human and must maintain his physical health as he grows older. The doctor is correct. David is human. I'm the alien. I live inside his head. I've invaded his body. I glow in the dark. My tentacles come out at night. One day David and I will leave this embattled world to take our rightful place in the universe.

~~~~~~~~~~~~~~~~~~~

GUARDIANS

APPENDIX

The Sexual Act of Integral Consensus and Genetic Disparity

Due to the altered conditions of genetic composition and chromosome disparity no act can be condoned or condemned. Sex is not a privilege -- it is a duty. Any representative of any species has the psychiatrically sanctified duty to exhibit sexual proclivity in any manner deemed essential to its extended pleasure. Sex must not be dictated by outmoded pseudo-puritan religious values. We live in an overpopulated world. Man is no longer the essential species. Therefore it is our scientific decision that society must incorporate diverse sexual patterns. Sex encourages the goals of modern society through diversification and self-alienation. Individuals of assorted species must be distended from self-action through sexual motivation to accelerate social programming. No species can altercate distinctive discrimination against any other species on the basis of sexual exclusion. All species naturally seek sexual integrity through harmonious promiscuity. No sex act is exclusive. Extreme sadomasochism in some organisms is a positive expansion of the conditioned behavioral response to survive in a counter-contingent environment. Certain sexual practices may lead to the total extinction of another indigenous group, but these practices are natural adaptations of the "survival instinct." The **Horg VII** master-species is an example of survival through sexual domination due to their peculiar predilection for human females. The Horg envelopes the female with gelatinous-foam regurgitated from an anus cavity. The foam acts like a sexual stimulant and the female is often dissolved in an after flow of acid. The experience is reported to be exquisite. The female does not cease to exist, but she is totally absorbed by the Horg VII.

In lieu of the above statements, every individual must be divested of all guilt regarding sexual activity. All species can live in sexually satisfying domesticity determined by stimulus-response triggers. Dominant sex-impulses will empirically resuscitate the social imbalance and encourage social relativism.